TEMPETE'S LEGACY

Emma Benham

ISBN

Hardcover: 978-1-965560-93-8
Paperback: 978-1-965560-94-5

Contents

Introduction

Tempête. The name itself whispers of monstrous change, a fitting moniker for the secret scientific project at the heart of this narrative. Set against the backdrop of the 1930s, a decade marked by both immense scientific strides and profound societal anxieties, Tempete's story unfolds as a chilling exploration of ambition, ethics, and the unintended consequences of pushing the boundaries of human potential. The story follows a group of brilliant but morally ambiguous scientists who, in their quest to conquer consumption, inadvertently unleash a force far beyond their comprehension: super-powered mutants. These individuals, forged in the crucible of secret experimentation and brutal military training, find themselves trapped in a web of conflicting loyalties and ethical dilemmas. Their powers, a testament to human ingenuity, become instruments of both defiance and oppression, forcing them to confront the profound moral implications of their existence. The central conflict between Thomas, the obedient soldier, and his former colleagues, the escaped mutants, fuels a high-stakes chase, a testament to the enduring strength of the human spirit in the face of adversity. The narrative is a reminder that even the most noble intentions can lead to catastrophic outcomes and that a strong moral compass must always guide the pursuit of progress.

Chapter 1: The Genesis of Tempête

The Parisian Laboratory

The air hung thick with the scent of ozone and antiseptic, a peculiar perfume clinging to the damp stone walls of the concealed laboratory. Hidden beneath the labyrinthine streets of 1930s Paris, nestled amongst forgotten catacombs and echoing cellars, lay the heart of Tempête. It wasn't a grand edifice boasting gleaming steel and humming machinery but rather a series of interconnected spaces cobbled together from repurposed industrial buildings and former wine cellars. The uneven cobblestone floors were slick with spilled chemicals, the air punctuated by the rhythmic hiss of pressure valves and the sporadic crackle of high-voltage discharges.

Dr. Dubois, a wiry man with eyes that held the weary intelligence of a seasoned scholar, oversaw the operation. His lab coat, perpetually stained with a kaleidoscope of chemicals, hung loosely on his frame, a testament to countless sleepless nights spent hunching over microscopes and Petri dishes. He was the driving force behind Tempête, his ambition fueled by a desperate desire to conquer the scourge of consumption, the "white plague" that stalked the city's underbelly. His colleagues, Dr. Moreau, a meticulous geneticist with a penchant for precision, and Dr. Petrova, a brilliant biochemist whose sharp intellect often clashed with Dubois's impulsive nature, shared his relentless drive. Dr. Thorne, a younger, more ethically hesitant physician, completed their clandestine team.

The laboratory was a chaotic symphony of scientific endeavor. Rows upon rows of test tubes, filled with bubbling concoctions of unknown substances, lined the workbenches. Glass beakers, some cracked and stained, contained viscous fluids of varying hues, ranging from the ethereal pale green of newly extracted serum to the ominous deep crimson of blood samples. The air vibrated with the low hum of centrifuges and the whirring of specialized equipment, meticulously crafted and repurposed from a variety of sources, a testament to the ingenuity of their covert operation. Every corner held a hint of the secret nature of their work: hidden compartments, concealed passages, and a network of secret tunnels beneath the cobbled streets that allowed for discreet entry and exit.

Their initial experiments were fraught with failure. Years were spent poring over microscopic slides, analyzing tissue samples, and painstakingly experimenting with various strains of bacteria and viruses. They explored the genetic makeup of patients with consumption, seeking a chink in the armor of the disease, a weakness they could exploit. The initial breakthroughs were alluring glimpses into the possibilities, offering hope that one day, they would achieve their ambitious goal. The team worked tirelessly, their dedication bordering on obsession, fueled by the tragic consequences of a disease that claimed countless lives, leaving a trail of grief and despair in its wake.

The breakthrough came unexpectedly. During a routine analysis of a patient's genetic material, a peculiar anomaly was detected – a previously unknown gene, dormant in the human genome, seemingly activated by the consumption bacteria itself. It was a mutation, a random twist of fate, yet it offered an unprecedented opportunity. Their initial hypothesis was that this gene was responsible for the body's defense mechanisms against the disease, amplified to an extreme degree by the harsh conditions of the infection. It represented not only a potential cure but something far more extraordinary.

The discovery ignited a wave of feverish activity within the laboratory. They isolated the gene, meticulously sequenced it, and began the demanding process of understanding its function. Their research delved into the realm of cellular biology, exploring the gene's interaction with other cellular processes and the mechanisms by which it manifested its unique properties. They found that the gene wasn't merely a defense mechanism; it was a powerful catalyst capable of manipulating cellular regeneration and enhancing physical capabilities beyond usual human limitations.

Their first test subject was Dmitri, a young man from the city's impoverished districts, consumed by the disease. His body, ravaged by the relentless onslaught of consumption, was a testament to the severity of the illness. They administered the modified gene using a novel method of gene therapy they had developed, and they waited, watched, and held their breath in anticipation. The process was slow and gradual, and the transformation was almost invisible at first. But soon, there were signs of improvement: His cough subsided, his fever broke, and most strikingly, his strength began to increase at an alarming rate.

Weeks turned into months, and Dmitri's transformation became undeniable. He possessed superhuman strength, his muscles rippling with phenomenal power. His healing capacity was equally astounding; wounds that would have been fatal to any ordinary man healed within hours, leaving barely a scar. The initial delight was quickly replaced by apprehension. They had created something extraordinary, something that lay far beyond their initial intention of finding a cure for consumption. They had created a superhuman.

The implications were staggering. The scientific world, if it ever learned of their discovery, would be thrown into chaos. Their work, a classified operation shrouded in secrecy, was now teetering on the edge of a seismic shift. Their quiet laboratory, a place dedicated to scientific pursuit, had become something far more sinister. They had ventured into uncharted territory and crossed a line they had not foreseen. The ethical ramifications loomed large.

As the weight of their discovery settled on their shoulders, a heavy burden pressed against their conscience. The air grew thick with a sense of unease, and the room seemed to darken with the weight of their moral dilemma. The faint scent of anxiety hung in the air, mingling with the sharp tang of regret. The weight of their actions seemed to whisper in their ears, a haunting reminder of the choices they had made.

The scientists debated fiercely, the weight of their creation pressing down on them. The potential benefits were immense, yet the risks were catastrophic. They knew that such a discovery could not remain hidden. The military, with its inherent appetite for power and weaponry, would undoubtedly be interested in their work. It was only a matter of time before their carefully guarded secret would be discovered.

Their fears materialized sooner than expected. A discreet visit from a high-ranking military officer, a man whose presence radiated authority and menace, brought the reality of their situation into sharp focus. He was interested not in curing consumption, but in weaponizing their creation, in harnessing the power they had unleashed. The initial reluctance of the scientists was met with a polite yet firm ultimatum: cooperate or face the consequences. The choice was presented not as an option but as an inevitable trajectory, shaping the future of Project Tempête in ways none of them could have anticipated. The laboratory, once a haven of scientific exploration, was now under the iron fist of the military, transforming into a crucible where science and military ambition would collide in a destructive dance.

Dmitris Awakening

The world swam back into focus in blurry, disorienting waves. Dmitri's eyelids fluttered open, met not by the comforting darkness of unconsciousness but by the harsh glare of a single bare bulb hanging precariously from the ceiling. His head throbbed a dull, persistent ache that resonated deep within his skull. He tried to move, to sit up, but his body felt heavy, unresponsive. A wave of nausea washed over him, forcing him to close his eyes again, the metallic tang of blood filling his mouth.

He'd been… different. He knew it instinctively, a visceral understanding that transcended the confusion clouding his mind. He remembered flashes of intense pain, of needles piercing his skin, of a chilling, almost unbearable cold that had settled deep within his bones. And then… nothing. A void. Now, this.

He opened his eyes again, this time focusing on his surroundings. He was lying on a narrow cot, the rough fabric scratching against his skin. The room was small and stark, its walls lined with shelves crammed with glass vials and strange, metallic instruments. The air hung heavy with the scent of antiseptic and something else… something harsh and unfamiliar, like burnt metal and ozone.

Panic clawed at his throat. He tried to speak, but only a raspy croak escaped his lips. His throat felt raw, his tongue thick and swollen. He shifted slightly, and a sharp pain shot through his left arm, causing him to gasp. He looked down and saw a bandage, stained a dark crimson.

He flexed his fingers, each movement accompanied by a dull ache. Then, hesitantly tried to sit up. The effort required seemed monumental, yet he did it. His muscles, usually weak and pliable, felt dense, powerful, almost alien. He stood, his legs surprisingly steady despite the throbbing in his head.

He took a tentative step, then another. He felt… strong. Immensely strong. A feeling unlike anything he'd ever experienced before. He walked towards the door, his steps echoing in the silent room. He gripped the metal doorknob, the strength in his hand surprising him. He pulled it open, expecting resistance, but the solid metal yielded to his grip with unsettling ease, bending slightly under his grasp.

The corridor outside was dimly lit, the only light emanating from a flickering gas lamp at its far end. The floor was cold and damp beneath his bare feet. He continued walking, drawn by an instinct he didn't understand, propelled by a newfound power that both exhilarated and terrified him.

He reached a heavy, steel door at the end of the corridor. It was sealed shut, but he didn't hesitate. He gripped the door, his fingers digging into the cold metal. He pushed. With a groan of protesting metal, the immense door buckled and swung inward, revealing a larger room beyond.

Inside, he saw men in white coats, their faces illuminated by the flickering lights. They turned, startled, their eyes widening in disbelief as they saw him. One of them, a woman with sharp, intelligent eyes, stepped forward. She spoke in rapid French, her words barely audible above the pounding of Dmitri's own heart.

He didn't understand most of what she said, but he understood the fear in her voice. He understood the way she stared at his hands, at his powerful physique, at the raw, untamed power radiating from him.

The weeks that followed were a blur of tests, experiments, and increasingly invasive procedures. They wanted to understand what had happened to him, to chart the limits of his newfound abilities. They ran endless tests, monitoring his strength, his reflexes, and his healing capabilities. He could lift objects many times his weight, his wounds healed instantly, and he possessed an almost superhuman endurance. His enhanced senses were extraordinary. He could hear a whisper from across a room and smell the faintest trace of scent in the air.

But the experiments weren't just physical. They began probing his mind, pushing him to his mental limits, testing the boundaries of his rapidly expanding consciousness. He felt as though they were peeling back layers of his soul, exposing raw nerves, forcing him to confront a depth of capacity he didn't know existed.

Sleep offered little respite, his dreams a confusing jumble of fragmented images and unsettling sensations. He dreamt of needles, of cold, and of a terrifying, overwhelming power that threatened to consume him. He woke with a gasp, his heart racing, the lingering taste of metallic blood on his tongue.

The scientists, while seemingly focused on the scientific marvel they had created, also exhibited a profound unease. Their initial euphoria at their success had given way to a simmering apprehension. They watched him with a mixture of fascination and fear, their expressions shifting from clinical observation to something akin to horrified awe.

Dmitri's feelings were a chaotic mix of confusion and growing dread. He had become something... more. Something other. His physical power was undeniable, a brutal strength that unnerved him as much as it exhilarated him. He yearned for normalcy, for a life before the experiments, but that life now seemed like a distant, fading dream. The new Dmitri was a paradox: powerful yet vulnerable, a scientific marvel trapped in a cage of his own making. He longed for understanding, for a connection to the world that now felt both alien and dangerously captivating. His enhanced senses intensified every fear, every uncertainty. He felt their apprehension as acutely as his own, and it served only to deepen his growing unease. He was a weapon. He knew it. And the feeling left him chilled to the bone.

The scientists observed his emotional turmoil with clinical detachment, but their eyes betrayed a certain sympathy, perhaps even regret. They were trapped, too, their creation a monstrous testament to their ambition. The line between scientific endeavor and reckless hubris had blurred, and they all knew it. They had unwittingly unleashed a force they could no longer control, and the consequences were only beginning to reveal themselves.

Dmitri, the first success of Tempête, was both a triumph and a terrifying warning. The shadows lurking in the corners of the laboratory, once merely symbolic, now held a tangible threat, mirroring the darkness that was slowly consuming Dmitri himself. The silence between them, broken only by the faint hum of unseen machinery, spoke volumes. They were all caught in a web of their own making, and the fate of them all hung precariously in the balance.

Military Intervention

The heavy oak door creaked open, revealing not the sterile white coats of the scientists but the sharp, unforgiving lines of military uniforms. Two men entered, their boots echoing ominously on the polished concrete floor. They were tall, imposing figures, their faces etched with the harsh realities of war, their eyes assessing the laboratory with a calculating gaze. One, a Colonel with a steely gaze and a neatly trimmed mustache, addressed Dr. Dubois, the lead scientist of Tempête.

"Dr. Dubois," the Colonel's voice was clipped, devoid of any warmth. "We have been monitoring your progress. The reports are... impressive." He paused; the silence was heavy with unspoken implications. "The Reich requires your expertise, your... creations."

Dr. Dubois, a man whose life had been dedicated to the pursuit of scientific knowledge, felt a cold dread grip his heart. He had envisioned Tempête as a sanctuary, a place where groundbreaking research could push the boundaries of human understanding. Now, it felt more like a cage, its walls closing in on him and his colleagues. He exchanged a worried glance with Dr. Moreau, whose usually jovial face was now pale and strained. Dr. Petrova, ever stoic, stood rigid, her expression unreadable. Only Dr. Thorne seemed unaffected, his usual detached demeanor shielding his emotions.

"We... we were hoping to continue our research independently," Dubois stammered, attempting to maintain a semblance of control. The Colonel's smirk was a chilling response.

"Independent research has its limitations," the Colonel replied, his voice hardening. "The Reich has needs that supersede your academic pursuits. We have witnessed the potential of your... subject, Dmitri. We require more. Many more."

The scientists knew resistance was futile. The military's presence was overwhelming; heavily armed soldiers stood guard outside the laboratory, their weapons glinting menacingly in the dim light. The illusion of control, the delicate balance they had maintained, shattered like fragile glass. Tempête was no longer their own.

The takeover was swift and brutal. The scientists, once masters of their domain, were reduced to mere technicians, their every move monitored, their research dictated by the military's cold, strategic goals. The once collaborative spirit that had fueled their work was replaced by fear and uncertainty. The military's presence was an oppressive blanket, suffocating the creative energy that had once thrived within those walls. Discussions were hushed, whispers replacing the vibrant debates that had once animated the laboratory.

The change in atmosphere was unmistakable. The comforting hum of scientific equipment was now overlaid by the constant, unsettling presence of armed guards patrolling the corridors. The once-sacred space was now a military facility, its original purpose – to conquer disease – twisted into a horrifying engine of war. The scientists were forced to increase the pace of their research, their efforts driven not by scientific curiosity but by the fear of the consequences of failure. The military's demands were relentless, their methods brutal.

The initial euphoria of their success with Dmitri, the thrill of pushing the boundaries of human potential, was now replaced by a profound sense of dread. They had created something extraordinary, but in doing so, they had unleashed a force they could not control. The ethical implications of their work, once a topic of thoughtful discussion, now loomed over them like a dark cloud, heavy with unspoken guilt.

The scientists' roles were redefined. They became mere cogs in a larger, far more sinister machine. They were given new directives and new subjects, but their autonomy was gone. The process of creating enhanced individuals was sped up, and a cold, efficient production line replaced the meticulous care and observation that had characterized their earlier work. The military's focus was solely on results, on quantifiable improvements, ignoring the potential human cost. The well-being of their creations became secondary to the demands of the war machine.

The scientists, particularly Dubois, wrestled with their consciences. They had hoped to alleviate human suffering, to cure disease. Now, their work was being twisted to inflict suffering, to create weapons of unimaginable power. Each successful creation – Irina, Thomas, Elara, Seraphina, and Marcus – was another nail in the coffin of their hopes. Their initial pride was replaced by a growing sense of guilt, a chilling awareness of the moral abyss they were plummeting into. The weight of their actions pressed heavily on their shoulders, an invisible burden that threatened to crush them.

The training regime implemented by the military was far more brutal than anything the scientists had foreseen. The mutants were pushed to their limits, their abilities honed into lethal weapons. There were casualties: individuals who broke under the pressure, their bodies failing under the relentless strain. The military showed no mercy; failure meant only one thing - termination. The scientists watched, powerless to intervene, as their creations were molded into instruments of war, their humanity eroded by the relentless demands of the military machine.

The shift from a scientific endeavor to a military operation was not just a change in setting; it was a profound shift in morality. The scientists, accustomed to the ethical guidelines of scientific research, now found themselves complicit in something far more sinister. The lines of their morality blurred their sense of self-questioning their very purpose. Were they heroes or villains? Scientists or architects of destruction? The answers eluded them, lost in the shadows of their creation.

The memory of Dmitri's strength, his raw power, haunted them. He was the proof of concept, the gateway to this new, terrifying reality. His screams during his initial training, barely audible over the hum of machinery, now echoed in their memories. Those screams were the premonition of a far larger tragedy. The faces of Irina, Thomas, Elara, Seraphina, and Marcus, each displaying a mixture of fear and forced compliance, haunted their waking hours. These were not merely test subjects anymore. They were children, products of their ambition, and now victims of a ruthless military machine.

The scientists' only solace was in their shared secret, their unspoken understanding of the ethical dilemma they were trapped in. Their secret meetings, once buzzing with excited discussions, now became somber gatherings where they silently acknowledged the weight of their responsibility and the monstrous implications of their creation. The initial optimism and ambition had been systematically eroded, leaving behind a shell of guilt and fear.

The military's iron grip tightened. Any attempts at dissent were swiftly crushed. The scientists knew their lives were at the mercy of the regime. Their work was no longer a pursuit of knowledge; it was a matter of survival. Tempête had become a prison, and they, the prisoners. Their only hope, a fragile, flickering flame in the darkness, rested in the possibility of escape, a desperate gamble that could either set them free or seal their fate. The future, once bright with the promise of scientific advancement, was now shrouded in the oppressive shadow of military intervention. The seeds of rebellion, though carefully concealed, were sown, waiting for the opportune moment to blossom into a desperate fight for survival, a desperate attempt to reclaim their humanity and undo the damage they had wrought.

The Creation Of The Others

The air crackled with a nervous energy, a stark contrast to the sterile efficiency of the laboratory. The scientists, their faces etched with a mixture of fear and grim determination, watched as Colonel Petrov barked orders through the reinforced concrete. Dmitri, the first success of Project Tempête, stood passively in the center of the room, his immense frame a testament to the project's terrifying potential. His eyes, though, held a haunted quality, a flicker of something akin to understanding in their depths. He was a creature of immense power but also a prisoner of it.

The next few years blurred into a relentless cycle of experimentation and brutal training. Dmitri, though powerful, was…simple. His raw strength was easily controlled, and his obedience drilled into him through methods that left even the hardened military men uneasy. It was clear more refined control was needed. More nuance. That is where Irina, Thomas, Elara, Seraphina, and Marcus entered the picture. They were the culmination of years of research, the refinement of a terrifying power.

Irina emerged first. Her mind was a whirlwind of information, a kaleidoscope of data processing at speeds that defied comprehension. She could absorb and process knowledge at an alarming rate, understanding complex equations and mastering intricate languages in a matter of hours. She was a walking library, a living computer, but her intellect was matched only by her intense, almost unsettling quiet. She observed everything, processed everything, and rarely spoke. Her eyes, however, held the weight of centuries of knowledge, a universe of unspoken thoughts swirling behind their piercing gaze. The scientists, used to raw power, were unnerved by the subtle, almost frightening control she possessed over the information itself.

Thomas, the next subject, presented a different challenge altogether. He wasn't as visibly imposing as Dmitri, but his enhanced senses made him a phantom, capable of perceiving the world in ways unimaginable to ordinary humans. He could hear a heartbeat across a crowded room, smell the faintest trace of fear on a person's breath, and sense subtle changes in temperature from miles away. His healing abilities were also extraordinary, faster, and more efficient than Dmitri's. But what set Thomas apart was his almost unnerving obedience. Unlike Dmitri, he displayed no hint of rebelliousness, his training seemingly perfecting the subservience ingrained within his enhanced physiology. He was the military's ideal weapon: cold, efficient, and utterly ruthless. This frightening compliance would later become a defining characteristic of his existence and a source of considerable anguish for the other Tempête subjects.

Elara was a storm contained within a fragile frame. She commanded the weather, manipulating atmospheric pressure, creating torrential downpours, or summoning blinding blizzards with barely a thought. Her moods mirrored her power: calm and serene one moment, a raging storm the next. She was unpredictable, her volatile temperament a reflection of her volatile abilities. The scientists struggled to control her, her very presence a chaotic force that defied even the most meticulously planned experiments. Her power was untamed, a force of nature in human form, capable of leveling cities or bringing life-giving rain to parched lands. This made her a compelling yet terrifying weapon.

Seraphina possessed the power of telepathy, a silent, invisible force that gave her access to the minds of others. She could read their thoughts, influence their decisions, and even implant suggestions. Her power was insidious, a constant reminder of the vulnerability of the human mind. Yet, unlike the others, Seraphina showed a deep empathy, a compassion that clashed violently with the cold, calculating nature of her abilities. She understood the pain and suffering of her fellow subjects and was often found trying to comfort them in the small ways she could, making her a double-edged sword for the military.

Finally, there was Marcus, a walking inferno. Pyrokinesis burned within him, a terrifying power that allowed him to manipulate flames with a flick of his wrist. He could conjure walls of fire, create searing blasts of heat, or reduce an entire building to ashes with a mere thought. He was volatile, impulsive, and dangerous, his temper as fiery as his abilities. Unlike the others, who showed at least moments of controlled composure, Marcus was a raging fire, barely contained within his own body. His unpredictable nature made him a liability in the eyes of the military, yet his power was too great to ignore.

The creation of these five mutants marked a turning point in Tempête. The scientists, initially driven by a desire to conquer disease, had unleashed a power that dwarfed their wildest expectations. Their work had become a weapon, a tool of war, wielded by a regime that cared little for the ethical considerations of their creation. The laboratory, once a sanctuary of scientific pursuit, had transformed into a cold, brutal training ground where these extraordinary individuals were molded into instruments of destruction. The scientists watched in helpless horror as their creations were stripped of their humanity, their potential for good forever overshadowed by the shadow of their destructive capabilities. The future, once a beacon of hope, was now a bleak and uncertain landscape dominated by the terrifying reality of their achievement. The lines between creator and created, between science and warfare, had become hopelessly blurred.

The creation of the others marked a dark chapter in the history of Tempête. Each of them possessed unique abilities, but they shared a common bond – the trauma of their creation and the subsequent ruthless exploitation at the hands of the military. The shadows of the war hung heavy over them, shaping their personalities and driving their actions in the years to come. Their escape, their struggle for survival, and the ultimate consequences of their existence would forever be interwoven with the tragic story of Tempête. The scientists, witnessing the creation of these individuals, understood they had crossed a line, a threshold that would forever separate them from the innocent ambitions that fueled their initial research. The innocence of scientific curiosity was lost, consumed by the grim realities of a world at war. The seeds of regret had been sown.

The Seeds of Rebellion

The rhythmic clang of steel on steel, the guttural shouts of instructors, and the stifled whimpers of pain formed a grim symphony within the walls of the military compound. This was the reality of life for Dmitri, Irina, Elara, Seraphina, and Marcus – a brutal ballet of obedience and coercion orchestrated by men who saw them not as individuals but as weapons to be sharpened. The initial awe that had greeted their emergence had long since faded, replaced by the cold, calculating gaze of military strategists.

Dmitri, with his superhuman strength, was forced to endure endless drills, his body pushed to the very brink of collapse. The rapid healing that was once a marvel now served only as a grotesque testament to his resilience, allowing him to endure punishment that would kill a normal man a hundred times over. He carried the weight of his immense power, a burden that crushed his spirit as surely as any physical torment. His eyes, once bright with the innocent wonder of discovery, were now clouded with a deep, unsettling weariness.

Irina, gifted with intellect far beyond her years, was subjected to a different kind of torture. Confined to a sterile room, she was forced to decode complex ciphers, her mind a battlefield where logic warred against the creeping despair of her situation. Sleep deprivation, sensory overload, and psychological manipulation were tools employed to break her, to reduce her brilliance to a mere instrument of military intelligence. The vast library of her mind, once a sanctuary of knowledge, was now a prison of her creation.

Elara, mistress of the weather, found her powers manipulated and controlled. Forced to conjure storms and manipulate atmospheric conditions, she became a living weapon of mass destruction, her inherent connection to the elements twisted into a means of terror. She felt the guilt, the burden of her power, but she could only express it through the raging storms she commanded, a silent scream against the cruelty inflicted upon her.

Seraphina's telepathic abilities were the most insidious weapon of all. The military used her to probe the minds of their enemies, to extract secrets, and to instill fear. She was forced to witness the darkest recesses of the human psyche, the horrors of war, and the bleakness of human depravity. The whispers of countless minds, the echoes of violence and hatred, bombarded her consciousness, slowly eroding her sanity. Her mind, a once clear spring, became a murky swamp of pain and despair.

Marcus, with his pyrokinetic gifts, was a walking inferno. He was trained to channel his fiery powers to unleash devastation with pinpoint accuracy. His control, though, was far from perfect. He was plagued by uncontrollable bursts of flame, a constant reminder of the terrifying force that lay within him. He lived in a world of searing heat and suffocating smoke, a perpetual prisoner of his being.

The seeds of rebellion were sown not in grand decrees or organized resistance but in the subtle acts of defiance, the quiet moments of shared understanding, and the slow, agonizing realization of their shared fate. It began with a look, a fleeting exchange of eyes, a silent nod of knowledge across a crowded training yard. The unspoken communication built a bridge between them, a connection forged in the crucible of shared suffering.

During a grueling training exercise, Dmitri pushed beyond his limits and accidentally unleashed a surge of power that caused a minor tremor in the earth. The tremor was subtle and easily dismissed as a natural occurrence, but it was enough to create a crack in the seemingly impenetrable facade of control. It was a small act of defiance, but it resonated deeply with the others, a silent testament to their shared strength and growing discontent.

Irina, during one of her exhausting decoding sessions, subtly altered a crucial piece of intelligence, deliberately misleading her military handlers. It was a tiny change, one that wouldn't be immediately noticed, but it planted a seed of doubt, a crack in the perfect system of control. It was an act of intellectual subversion, a subtle rebellion against the intellectual oppression she endured.

Elara, during one of her weather manipulation sessions, subtly altered the wind currents during a live-fire exercise, causing a minor disruption. It wasn't enough to derail the exercise but enough to demonstrate that even their powers could be subtly used against their captors. A brief rain shower unexpectedly cooled off a sweltering training area which acted as her silent protest.

Seraphina, in her nightly torment of extracted intelligence, subtly planted suggestions of dissent in the minds of those tasked with controlling them. Subtle phrases of doubt, whispers of defiance, carefully inserted into the subconscious of their guards – a slow, deliberate poisoning of their overseers' minds. It was a slow, gradual subversion, but the effects would be profound over time.

Marcus, during a demonstration of his pyrokinetic abilities, allowed a small flicker of uncontrolled flame to escape, briefly singeing the uniform of a particularly cruel instructor. It was a small, almost accidental act, but the fear in the instructor's eyes, the unintended consequence, was a small victory, a tiny step towards breaking free.

These seemingly insignificant acts were far from random; they were signs of a simmering resentment, of a growing awareness of their shared defeat. They were the whispers of rebellion, the emerging stirrings of defiance that would soon erupt into a full-blown fight for freedom. The bond of shared trauma and suffering had become a foundation for a growing unity, an implicit rebellion against their oppressors. They were learning to communicate, to trust, to strategize, all while navigating the treacherous waters of their captivity.

The military, however, remained oblivious to these subtle acts of rebellion, blinded by their hubris and convinced of their complete control. They failed to recognize the quiet strength that simmered beneath the surface, the growing resolve that would ultimately lead to their downfall. They had created monsters, yes, but they had also inadvertently forged a bond between them, a unity that would challenge their very authority. The seeds of rebellion had been planted, nurtured in the dark soil of oppression, and they were now ready to sprout. The military's complacency, their blindness to the subtle signs of rebellion, proved to be their greatest weakness. Their confidence in their superior power masked a deeper vulnerability, a simplicity that would soon be exposed.

The scientists, watching from the sidelines, a mixture of guilt and fear gnawing at their consciences, observed this slow, simmering rebellion with a mixture of horror and hope. They had created these beings, and now they bore witness to their agonizing struggle for freedom. They understood the monstrous implications of their creations, yet they also secretly admired the courage of their unwilling subjects, the growing spark of rebellion in their hearts. The scientists' initial regret had transformed into a more complex emotion – a profound sense of responsibility, a deep sense of accountability for the suffering they had unleashed. Their silence and inaction had contributed to the horrific suffering of the mutants. They wondered if it was too late to redeem themselves. The fate of Tempête, its creators, and its creations hung dangerously in the balance, poised on the knife edge between destruction and potential, yet uncertain, redemption. The stage was set; the rebellion was about to begin.

Chapter 2: Weaponization and Escape

Rigorous Training

The air hung thickly with the stench of sweat, blood, and disinfectants. The cavernous training facility, carved from the bowels of a repurposed munitions factory outside of Lyon, echoed with the rhythmic thud of impact and the screams of exertion. This wasn't merely training; it was systematic dehumanization, a brutal process designed to break the will of the mutants and forge them into weapons.

For Dmitri, the behemoth of a man, the training focused on raw, destructive power. He spent hours each day smashing concrete blocks, tearing steel bars, and enduring blows from specially designed impact weapons that would have shattered the bones of a normal man. His regenerative abilities were a double-edged sword; they allowed him to withstand the punishment, but they also meant the cycle of pain continued, endlessly testing the limits of his endurance. The psychological torment was far more subtle, a constant barrage of verbal abuse designed to strip him of his identity, reducing him to a brute force, a mere instrument of war.

Irina, with her unparalleled intellect, faced a different kind of torture. Confined to a small, dimly lit room, she was subjected to relentless interrogation and mental puzzles designed to break her concentration and push her to the brink of madness. Sleep deprivation was a constant companion, replaced only by grueling exercises designed to test her physical stamina – a cruel irony, given her mind was the weapon they sought to harness. The goal was to ensure her immense intellect remained at their disposal, a tool to be wielded at will, regardless of her desires or moral compunctions.

Thomas, already conditioned to obedience, experienced a different form of torture. His enhanced senses, once a source of wonder, became instruments of his tormentors. He was forced to endure amplified sounds, blinding flashes of light, and a constant bombardment of excruciating smells and tastes. His heightened empathy was weaponized, forcing him to bear witness to the suffering of others, compounding his emotional turmoil. They honed his already exceptional healing capabilities through systematic injury and forced regeneration, a process more akin to vivisection than training.

Elara's training was a terrifying dance with the elements. She was forced to control her power in environments designed to push her to her absolute limits. Extreme temperatures, unpredictable winds, and relentless storms tested the boundaries of her abilities, culminating in forced weather manipulation that bordered on meteorological terrorism. The drills were aimed at making her a weapon of mass destruction, erasing her from her capacity for empathy and replacing it with the sterile obedience of a programmed drone.

Seraphina, with her telepathic gifts, endured a different kind of hell. They attempted to exploit her abilities for surveillance and espionage, forcing her to endure the mental chaos of multiple synchronized voices, invasive probes into her thoughts, and relentless interrogation at the level of her consciousness. This psychic torture was aimed at both controlling and weaponizing her natural capacity for communication. The constant invasion of her mind was designed to break her spirit and leave her a hollow shell, a vessel for their strategic intentions.

Marcus, the pyrokinetic, suffered the most visceral form of torment. His training involved controlling flames at ever-increasing temperatures and magnitudes, pushing him to the precipice of self-immolation. The burns, while quickly healing, left scars both physical and emotional, a constant reminder of his power and the vulnerability that came with it. Every session was a controlled test of endurance. The fear of losing control, of accidentally incinerating himself or others, added a layer of psychological torture to his physical suffering.

The training wasn't just physical and mental; it was designed to break their sense of self to replace their identities with programmed obedience. They were deprived of sleep, subjected to starvation diets, and kept in isolation for extended periods, undermining their ability to trust anyone, including each other. The goal wasn't merely to control their powers; it was to control their very souls.

The brutality wasn't random; it was meticulously planned. Each mutant underwent a tailored training regimen designed to exploit their strengths while simultaneously breaking their will. The military psychologists, detached and cold, meticulously charted their progress, measuring their resilience and obedience with clinical precision. Their charts were a testament to systematic dehumanization, the systematic stripping of personality, turning of human beings into weapons.

The escape, when it finally came, was not a spontaneous act of rebellion but a carefully orchestrated strategy masterminded by Irina. She used her exceptional intellect to exploit the weaknesses in the security protocols, identifying the blind spots in the system, the vulnerabilities in the guards' routines, and the subtle cracks in the fortress's seemingly impenetrable structure. She meticulously planned every detail, anticipating every possible contingency and using her skills to manipulate her fellow mutants to cooperate subtly.

The training, however brutal, had inadvertently given them an advantage. The relentless physical and mental challenges had pushed them to the edge of their abilities, forcing them to understand and control their powers fully. Dmitri's strength was honed, Irina's intellect sharpened, Thomas's senses amplified, Elara's weather manipulation refined, Seraphina's telepathy heightened, and Marcus's control over fire solidified. The very brutality that sought to break them had ultimately made them stronger, more cunning, and more resourceful. The systematic torture and endless drills had forged an unwavering resolve among them.

The escape itself was a chaotic ballet of superhuman abilities. Dmitri smashed through reinforced doors, using his sheer strength to create a path of destruction. Irina used her intelligence to disable security systems and reroute power sources. Thomas utilized his heightened senses to anticipate and evade patrols. Elara manipulated the weather, creating blinding storms and torrential downpours to obscure their movements. Seraphina used her telepathy to communicate silently and sow confusion among the guards. Marcus deployed strategically placed blasts of fire to disable obstacles and create diversionary tactics.

The aftermath was a whirlwind of chaos. The escape triggered a massive manhunt as the military scrambled to recapture the escaped mutants. Tempete's facilities were thrown into disarray; the scientists, already grappling with the ethical implications of their work, were now confronted with the consequences of their creation. The escape was a resounding blow to the military's confidence and a stark reminder of the unpredictable nature of their experiments. It cast a shadow over their research, throwing the future of the program into disarray and sending shockwaves through the highest levels of power. The carefully constructed order had been broken; chaos reigned. The hunt for the escaped mutants had begun.

Irina's Strategic Planning

The cold, damp stone of the cell pressed against Irina's cheek. Five years. Five years later, she'd endured the brutal regimen, the relentless psychological conditioning, the endless drills designed to crush her spirit and mold her into a weapon. But the very intellect that made her a target also served as her salvation. While others succumbed to despair or outright madness, Irina meticulously charted a path to freedom, a plan built not on brute force but on calculated risk and intricate manipulation.

Her escape wasn't a spontaneous act of rebellion; it was a meticulously orchestrated ballet of deception. She began by subtly influencing the guards, playing on their prejudices and insecurities. A carefully placed comment here, a strategically leaked piece of information there – subtle nudges that eroded their discipline, creating cracks in the seemingly impenetrable fortress of military control. She studied their routines, their habits, their blind spots. She learned their names, their families, and their fears. She even managed to cultivate a semblance of trust, a fragile bond that would later prove crucial to her plan.

This wasn't merely about escaping her cell; it was about coordinating the escape of her fellow mutants. She understood that their individual strengths, while formidable, were insufficient to overcome the sheer military might arrayed against them. A coordinated effort was essential, and for that, she needed communication. She'd discovered a hidden ventilation shaft during her initial imprisonment, a pathway she surmised would lead to other parts of the facility. It was risky – a single misstep could mean recapture or worse – but it was the only viable method of communication within the heavily fortified complex.

Over weeks, months even, she used tiny scraps of paper, painstakingly written on in the faint moonlight filtering through the ventilation shafts, to send coded messages. Each message was a calculated risk, balanced against the urgency of their situation. The messages detailed the escape plan, assigning roles, outlining escape routes, and establishing rendezvous points. She appealed to their shared sense of injustice, their collective hatred of their captors. Elara, with her ability to control the weather, could create diversions. Marcus, with his pyrokinesis, could provide cover. Seraphina, with her telepathy, could provide crucial reconnaissance. Even Dmitri's brute strength, controlled and channeled, would be an invaluable asset. She needed them all to trust her, to believe in her plan, and to coordinate their efforts with flawless precision. Trust, in this context, was a luxury they couldn't afford.

The escape itself was a masterpiece of chaos and control. Elara, following Irina's instructions, triggered a fierce thunderstorm, short-circuiting the electrical grid and plunging the facility into darkness. The ensuing panic created a perfect smokescreen for their coordinated break. While the guards were scrambling to restore order, Marcus unleashed a wave of carefully controlled flames, creating diversions and blocking escape routes for their pursuers. The heat and smoke were disorienting, giving them the time they needed to navigate the maze of corridors and tunnels. Dmitri, meanwhile, cleared their path with a series of well-placed blows, creating openings and destroying obstacles. Seraphina, using her telepathic abilities, monitored the movement of the guards, guiding her colleagues through the labyrinthine facility.

Irina herself was at the heart of the operation, guiding the movements of her teammates, anticipating their every move, and reacting to unforeseen circumstances with a calm and methodical efficiency that contradicted the dangerous chaos surrounding them. She knew that any hesitation, any moment of weakness, would be fatal. The slightest slip would expose them all. Her mind worked with a cold, calculating precision, dissecting each obstacle, anticipating each reaction, and executing her plan with deadly efficiency. Every action was choreographed, every step precisely measured, creating a whirlwind of controlled chaos.

Their final rendezvous point was a hidden tunnel leading to the sewers beneath Lyon. The escape wasn't without casualties.

One guard, alerted by a stray spark from Marcus's powers, caught sight of Dmitri. A fierce struggle ensued; Dmitri caught off guard, was injured, his superhuman healing abilities taxed but not defeated. The escape was close, a hair's range from failure.

The foul-smelling sewers provided a difficult but safe passage to the outside. The stench of decay and filth was overpowering, but Irina pushed onward, her mind fixed on the freedom that lay just beyond. The tunnels, barely large enough to crawl through, offered little respite. Yet, as they emerged from the darkness and into the labyrinthine alleys of Lyon under the cover of the still-raging storm, a wave of relief washed over them. They were free. But freedom was just the beginning. The military wouldn't let them go so easily. The hunt was far from over.

Irina, though physically unharmed, bore the scars of her imprisonment. The psychological trauma was deeply ingrained, a constant companion. The memory of the brutal experiments, the relentless conditioning, and the dehumanization process haunted her waking thoughts and haunted her sleep. But she was not broken. The resilience forged in the crucible of her imprisonment had only hardened her resolve. Now, her intelligence and strategic prowess were directed toward survival, toward ensuring the safety of her companions, toward building a life beyond the reach of their pursuers. The escape was a victory, a testament to her unwavering will, a prelude to a larger battle yet to come.

Her immediate priority was securing safe havens. She knew the military would be using all available resources to track them down – facial recognition, DNA profiling, and every other technological tool at their disposal. Irina used her knowledge of hidden networks and underground safe houses, gleaned from years of covert observation and meticulous study. Her plan relied on creating a series of safe houses – secure locations that would allow them to regroup, recover, and plan their next move.

This new phase wouldn't be a simple case of hiding in plain sight. This would require deception on a grand scale, the creation of false identities, manipulating information flows, and using her exceptional intellect to outwit the considerable resources arrayed against them. She needed to think ahead, anticipating the moves of the military, creating a series of traps and misdirection to throw them off their trail. She was playing a deadly game of cat and mouse, but this time, she was the cat. Each move had to be calculated; each deception was meticulously planned. This was a war of wits, a battle fought not with weapons but with brains and strategy.

Their escape was only the first act in a much larger drama. The hunt for the Tempête mutants had just begun. Irina, the mastermind of the escape, understood this. She knew that the fight for survival had only just begun, and she was ready. The years of brutal training, the relentless conditioning, hadn't broken her. They had forged her into something stronger, something more resourceful, something far more dangerous. She would use her unique gifts not only to survive but also to ensure the survival of her colleagues. And perhaps even to exact some measure of revenge on the institution that had created them. The hunt was on, and Irina was prepared to play the long game. Her intelligence, her strategic thinking, and her unwavering determination would be their weapons. The fight for survival was a battle of wits, and Irina was ready to wage war. The fight had begun.

The Great Escape

The heavy oak door creaked open, revealing not the expected guard but a dimly lit corridor. Irina, her eyes gleaming with a calculated intensity, gestured silently to Elara. A subtle shift in the air pressure, almost imperceptible, announced Elara's power. A gust of wind, whipped up by her manipulation of the elements, slammed the door shut with a resounding boom, effectively sealing their escape route and masking the sound of their departure.

Marcus, his face a mask of controlled fury, was already halfway down the corridor, his bare hands crackling with barely contained energy. He moved like a phantom, a blur of motion, his pyrokinetic abilities subtly disabling the security cameras along their path. The heat radiating from him was intense, but he maintained precise control, ensuring that only the cameras were targeted, leaving the corridor itself unscathed. He moved with a terrifying grace, his movements a deadly dance between destruction and precision. A testament to the brutal training he'd endured. The heat was a shield, a warning, and a weapon all rolled into one.

Seraphina, her face pale but resolute, remained at the rear, her telepathic abilities working overtime. She shielded their minds from the inevitable search party, weaving a deceptive web of false impressions and planting suggestions of their escape in locations far removed from their actual position. Her power was a subtle art, requiring incredible concentration and mental stamina, a constant battle against the encroaching panic and the weight of responsibility for her fellow escapees. The mental strain was immense, a burden she bore silently, her serene exterior masking the ferocious struggle within. Each moment was a delicate dance on the precipice of exposure.

Thomas, though present, remained a silent observer, his enhanced senses picking up the slightest shift in the environment, every creak of the floorboards, every whispered conversation far beyond the capabilities of a normal human. While his loyalty to the military remained a chilling uncertainty, his exceptional abilities served as an invaluable asset to the escape. His presence was a double-edged sword, a potential savior and a looming threat all at once, a fact not lost on his former colleagues. The silence was his shield, his enhanced senses constantly monitoring their surroundings for the slightest anomaly, his loyalty to his former commanders a question mark hanging over their desperate flight.

Irina, leading the group, navigated the labyrinthine corridors with an unnerving ease. She knew the layout of the facility better than most of the guards, having used her intelligence not just for planning the escape but for mapping out the very structure of their prison. Her steps were measured, and each decision was carefully weighed and executed with deadly precision. Her mind worked like a finely tuned engine, constantly calculating probabilities, assessing risks, and anticipating countermeasures. She was the architect of their escape, a strategist who'd meticulously planned every detail, anticipating every possible obstacle and weaving their escape around them. The pressure was immense, and the consequences of failure were catastrophic.

Their path wasn't straightforward. They had to avoid patrolling guards, navigate complex security systems, and overcome multiple obstacles designed to trap and contain them. Each mutant used their unique abilities in a coordinated assault on the facility's defenses. Elara created diversions, conjuring powerful gusts of wind that forced doors open or scattered unsuspecting guards. Marcus burned through obstacles, creating paths where none existed. Seraphina neutralized any stray patrols or potential witnesses, obscuring their actions from prying minds. Thomas's enhanced senses guided them, providing advance warning of approaching danger. Irina orchestrated it all, the silent conductor of a deadly symphony of escape.

The escape stretched on for what felt like an eternity, a tense and harrowing sequence of near misses and daring maneuvers. The facility's alarm system was triggered countless times, setting off a cacophony of sirens and shouts. Still, the mutants, guided by

Irina's plan and using their combined abilities, managed to slip through the gaps, always a step ahead of their pursuers. The weight of their pursuers was immense, the potential for failure catastrophic. Yet Irina's plan, intricate and well thought out, remained flawless.

As they reached the outer perimeter, they were faced with their final hurdle – a heavily guarded gate. This was where Irina's ingenuity truly shone. Using a combination of telepathic suggestions from Seraphina and a meticulously crafted distraction orchestrated by Elara, Irina managed to create enough chaos to allow them to slip past the gate unnoticed. The guards, confused and disoriented, were left wondering what had happened, their minds filled with false memories and contradictory perceptions.

Once outside, the mutants were free, but their freedom was short-lived. The world outside was no less dangerous than the one they'd just escaped. The military, alerted to the breach, was already mobilizing its forces to recapture them. Their escape was only the beginning of a much larger, far more dangerous game. But they had tasted freedom, a taste that would fuel their fight for survival. The escape was a testament to their courage, their combined strength, and their unwavering resolve to fight for their freedom.

The night air was cold and crisp as they fled into the darkness, their escape a testament to their coordinated efforts, each mutant playing a vital role in their successful flight. Irina's sharp intellect, Elara's control over the elements, Marcus's raw destructive power, Seraphina's subtle mental manipulation, and Thomas's heightened senses - all combined to create a formidable force that even the military's rigorous security couldn't contain. Yet, despite their successful escape, a shadow of doubt remained. The world outside was not a sanctuary, merely a new battleground where their powers would be both their strength and their curse. The fight for their lives had just begun. They were free but not safe. The pursuit had merely shifted from the sterile confines of their prison to the unforgiving expanse of the world.

They moved swiftly, their destination unknown, their future uncertain. The freedom they had won was fragile, a precarious balance between hope and despair. The immediate concern was survival; the larger question was their purpose. Were they merely escapees, fleeing from a deadly past, or were they something more? Each of them wrestled with this question. Irina felt the weight of leadership pressing upon her, the responsibility of her team's safety heavy on her shoulders. Elara's power held the potential for immense destruction, and she struggled with her guilt. Marcus's anger was a constant threat, a burning ember waiting to ignite into a raging inferno. Seraphina's mind, constantly bombarded by sensory information, was fatigued, yet her telepathic abilities were crucial. Thomas, a silent enigma, held the key to their potential demise. His allegiance remained a mystery that cast a long, cold shadow over their escape. The escape was a success; their future was anything but certain. The game was far from over. The hunt continued.

The Aftermath

The echoing silence that followed the slammed door was a deceptive calm. The air crackled with unspoken tension, the weight of their audacious escape pressing down on them like a physical burden. Irina, ever the strategist, had already begun formulating their next move. Her escape plan, meticulously crafted over months of painstaking observation and calculated risks, had hinged on exploiting the inherent flaws in the military's security protocols – flaws she'd discovered through her relentless analysis of their routines and vulnerabilities. But this was only the first step. The military wouldn't simply shrug and accept their loss. Retribution was inevitable.

The first sign of the military's reaction was subtle. A barely perceptible shift in the electromagnetic field, picked up by Elara's acutely sensitive perception. She felt it – a ripple in the air, a disturbance in the balance of the natural world, indicative of a technologically enhanced search party. Unseen drones, equipped with advanced sensory technology, were already scanning the city, their presence felt rather than seen. Irina, eyes narrowed, confirmed Elara's sensing. Their escape, while successful, had left a trace – a digital footprint in the vast network of surveillance systems.

The city, a labyrinth of twisting streets and shadowed alleys, became their sanctuary and their cage. Their pursuers were not simply soldiers; they were highly trained specialists equipped with technology far surpassing anything the civilian world possessed. They were hunting not just for escapees but for weapons – weapons of unimaginable power. The weight of this realization settled heavily upon them. They were hunted not only for their abilities but because of them. Their very existence posed a threat.

Marcus, his pyrokinetic abilities simmering just beneath the surface, was a walking powder keg. His frustration fueled his anger, threatening to erupt at any moment. The restraint he displayed was a testament to the iron will Irina had managed to instill in him during their covert planning sessions. His fiery nature was a double-edged sword, a potent weapon but also a dangerous liability. One wrong move, one spark of uncontrolled rage, and their cover would be blown. He was a living embodiment of the project's dark side.

Seraphina's telepathic abilities, once a source of comforting connection, were now a constant burden. The cacophony of thoughts, fears, and anxieties of the city swirled around her, a storm raging within her mind. She was privy to the panicked whispers of the civilians, the cold, calculating strategy of their pursuers, and the gnawing fear of her own team. The constant influx of information threatened to overwhelm her, draining her energy and compromising her focus. She was a sponge, soaking up every thought, every emotion. The silence, the brief moments of quiet, were a welcome relief.

Irina sought refuge in her intellectual pursuits. Even in the midst of their desperate flight, her brilliant mind worked tirelessly, analyzing the weaknesses of their pursuers and devising countermeasures. She recognized the strategic importance of maintaining a low profile, of disappearing into the city's anonymity. Her intellectual capabilities were not just a means of survival; they were their greatest strength. The information gleaned through her cunning analyses guided their every step.

Elara, the weather manipulator, had her own unique burden. The guilt of her immense power weighed heavily on her. Each gust of wind, each shift in atmospheric pressure, carried a reminder of the potential for devastation within her. The thought of causing harm, of using her powers against innocent bystanders, haunted her, adding another layer of complexity to their desperate flight. She yearned for a peaceful life, a quiet corner where she could harness her abilities without fear of unleashing chaos.

The fallout within Tempête was as devastating as the military's response. The escape of the mutants had left a gaping hole in the organization, a wound that festered with betrayal and uncertainty. The remaining scientists, those who had not participated in the escape, were consumed by fear and paranoia. The trust that had once been the cornerstone of their clandestine operation had crumbled, leaving only suspicion and self-preservation. Their shared secret, their collective guilt, had become a chasm dividing them, threatening to tear apart the fabric of their once-united enterprise.

Dr. Reed, the sole remaining scientist clinging to the belief in their work, was left to grapple with the implications of his creation. His unshakeable faith in the potential of enhanced individuals, however misguided, had driven him forward, even as the consequences of his actions unfolded around him. The escape was not merely a setback; it was a catastrophic failure of his vision. His unwavering conviction, once a beacon, now cast a long, dark shadow over his future. He would press on, he resolved, to continue the work, to perfect the process, to achieve his goal of creating a new breed of superior human beings. The ethical questions were a distant whisper compared to the thunder of his ambition.

The military's response was swift and brutal. A city-wide manhunt was launched, targeting not just the escapees but anyone suspected of aiding them. The once clandestine operation of Tempête was now public knowledge, a stain upon the military's reputation. The consequences extended beyond the immediate aftermath of the escape; it rippled through the social fabric of the city, creating fear, distrust, and suspicion. The military's grip tightened, its methods becoming increasingly harsh. The city was turned into a hunting ground, a silent battleground where the hunters and the hunted moved like shadows in the night.

The escapees were not merely fugitives; they were symbols of a larger failure, a testament to the unchecked ambition of science and the destructive potential of military power. Their flight was a desperate struggle for survival, a desperate plea for a world that refused to accept their existence. They were not just victims; they were the living consequences of a reckless experiment, a tragic byproduct of the relentless pursuit of scientific advancement at any cost. They were the ghosts of their own creation, forever haunted by the past and uncertain of the future.

The city, once a vibrant center of life and industry, now held its breath, a collective gasp caught in its throat. The pervasive fear was unmistakable, a chilling reminder of the power wielded by those who controlled the levers of both science and military might. The escape had shattered the fragile illusion of safety, leaving behind a city teetering on the brink of chaos. The hunt continued, not merely for the escapees, but for something far more elusive — a sense of order, a semblance of control in a world forever altered by the audacious experiment known as Tempête. The long shadow of their escape stretched into the unknown, promising more bloodshed and more upheaval. This relentless pursuit mirrored the relentless march of scientific progress and the ever-present threat of unchecked ambition. The true aftermath would only be revealed in time.

Thomas's Loyalty

The train rattled, a metallic tremor that vibrated through Thomas's enhanced senses. He sat rigidly, his eyes scanning the compartment, his ears straining for any unusual sound. Even the rhythmic clatter of the wheels was a symphony of potential threats. Five years. Five years he had spent chasing ghosts, the spectral remnants of his former colleagues, the other Tempête escapees. Five years of unwavering loyalty to the institution that had created him, shaped him, weaponized him. The memory of his training still stung, a constant ache beneath the surface of his enhanced perception.

He remembered the cold, sterile rooms of the facility, the relentless drills, and the excruciating physical conditioning designed to push his body and his mind to their absolute limits. He recalled the burning pain of his accelerated healing, a constant reminder of the unnatural power coursing through his veins. He remembered the faces of his instructors, hard, unforgiving men who saw him not as a person but as an instrument of war. He was a weapon honed to deadly precision, and his purpose was clear: hunt down the others, bring them back, or eliminate them if necessary.

The military's training hadn't just enhanced his physical capabilities; it had honed his mind, sharpening his instincts, his intuition, and his ability to anticipate danger before it manifested. He was a predator, trained to track, to stalk, to kill. Every sound, every scent, every fleeting shadow was meticulously analyzed and filtered through the enhanced lenses of his perception. He was a ghost himself, moving through the world undetected, his presence a subtle shift in the air, a faint tremor in the stillness.

His mission was absolute, a chilling decree etched into the very core of his being. Doubt, hesitation, empathy – these were luxuries he couldn't afford. They were weaknesses to be purged, emotions to be suppressed, and vulnerabilities to be exploited by his enemies. The escapees were traitors, deserters, and threats to national security. He had been trained to see them as such, and his programming, ingrained through years of rigorous conditioning, allowed no room for dissent.

But beneath the surface, a flicker of something else burned. A faint ember of something that refused to be extinguished. It wasn't rebellion, not quite. It was more like… curiosity. A nagging question, a whisper in the quiet moments when his mind momentarily slipped free from the chains of his programming. He saw snippets, fragments of memories, of his life before the experiments, before the training, before his transformation into a weapon. Fleeting images: laughter, warmth, a feeling of belonging. They were blurry and indistinct, but their presence was undeniable.

The memories were like shards of glass, painful yet oddly alluring. They hinted at a life beyond the relentless pursuit, beyond the blood-soaked path he was forced to tread. They were a stark contrast to the cold, sterile reality of his current existence, a tantalizing glimpse into a world where empathy, compassion, and human connection were not weaknesses but strengths.

On this particular mission, Thomas was tracking Elara. Her ability to manipulate the weather was a powerful weapon capable of inflicting widespread devastation. Intelligence suggested she was seeking refuge in a remote mountain range, a region known for its unpredictable weather patterns – a perfect hiding place for someone with Elara's powers.

The journey was arduous. Thomas traversed treacherous terrain, his enhanced senses constantly alert, his body adapting effortlessly to the changing altitude and temperature. His healing factor was a constant companion, mending the minor injuries that inevitably occurred during his relentless pursuit. He followed the subtle clues Elara had left behind – a disrupted weather pattern, an unusual gust of wind, a faint trace of her scent carried on the mountain breeze. He was a hunter, guided by instinct and honed by years of brutal training.

As he neared his destination, the weather turned ferocious. A blizzard raged around him, a swirling vortex of snow and ice. But the storm was not an obstacle; it was a challenge. He reveled in its ferocity, embracing the biting wind and the stinging snow as a testament to his enhanced endurance. The storm was merely another element to master, another challenge to overcome in his relentless pursuit.

He found Elara in a secluded cave, huddled beneath a thick blanket of furs. She was weak, exhausted, her power seemingly drained. He approached her cautiously, his senses heightened, expecting a sudden burst of energy, a display of her weather-controlling abilities. But there was no resistance, no fight. Only a fragile, vulnerable woman, her eyes filled with a mixture of fear and resignation.

For the first time in five years, Thomas hesitated. He saw not a traitor, not a threat, but a fellow victim of Tempête, a creature warped and altered by the same cruel science that had molded him. He saw a reflection of his own past, a glimpse of the humanity he had been forced to suppress. The hesitation, however, was fleeting. His training kicked in, overriding the fleeting doubt. He moved forward, his hand reaching for the weapon concealed beneath his cloak.

The weapon was a specially designed serum, a memory-erasing agent, a tool designed to break the will of the escapees, to eliminate their individuality and, thus, their rebellious spirit. The military believed that by erasing their memories, they could reclaim their assets and neutralize their threat. Thomas knew this – he was intimately familiar with the serum's effects. He'd seen its effect on those who had resisted. Their eyes were vacant, the light of their humanity extinguished.

He looked at Elara, her vulnerability a stark contrast to the turbulent power she commanded. His hand trembled slightly, a minuscule tremor that betrayed the conflict raging within him. He knew what he was supposed to do. He knew the consequences of failure. But a flicker of defiance, faint but persistent, threatened to shatter the fragile façade of his programmed obedience. The hunt was far from over. And the hunt was not just for the other escapees. It was also for something more elusive: Thomas's own identity, his own humanity, and perhaps, the tiniest sliver of hope for a life beyond the brutal efficiency of the military machine. His loyalties were about to face their ultimate test. The question was, which loyalty would prevail? The loyalty to the military, the loyalty to the mission, or the loyalty to the faint whisper of his own forgotten humanity.

Chapter 3: The Hunt Begins

Thomas's Pursuit

The Parisian rain hammered against the corrugated iron roof of the abandoned factory, a relentless rhythm mirroring the relentless pursuit in Thomas's heart. Five years. Five years since the escape, five years since the order was given, five years he had hunted his former colleagues, his fellow… creations. The scent of damp earth and decaying metal filled his nostrils, a familiar olfactory landscape that spoke of hidden things, shadows, and secrets. His enhanced senses, a cruel gift from Tempête, amplified every nuance, every tremor of movement in the derelict building before him. He could hear the faintest whisper of conversation, the subtle shift of weight on the dilapidated floorboards.

He'd tracked them here, to the forgotten outskirts of Lyon. Irina, the mastermind, is always a step ahead, always leaving a breadcrumb trail just tantalizing enough to keep him on the chase. This time, however, felt different. The air thrummed with nervous energy, a palpable tension that spoke not only of fear but of something more potent, something… expectant.

His enhanced healing abilities, a constant hum beneath his skin, were a constant reminder of his unnatural existence. A bullet graze, a broken bone, even a deep gash, would heal in hours, leaving little more than a faint scar. This resilience, this almost inhuman fortitude, was a double-edged sword. It fueled his relentless pursuit, but it also left him acutely aware of his own monstrous nature. He wasn't human, not entirely. He was a weapon, honed and sharpened by the military, his every instinct tuned to kill.

He moved through the shadows, a phantom in the rain-slicked alleys, his heightened hearing picking up the sounds of scurrying rats and the distant rumble of a passing tram. The factory was a labyrinth, a decaying monument to a forgotten industry, filled with the ghosts of workers past and the echoing whispers of the present. He navigated the maze with practiced ease, his senses guiding him towards the heart of the building, where the air grew thick with the scent of woodsmoke and something else... something metallic, almost... electrical.

The scent led him to a vast, cavernous space, once a factory floor, now cluttered with makeshift beds, cooking fires, and the tools of survival. Four figures huddled around a flickering lamp, their faces illuminated in the unsteady light. Irina, her sharp eyes radiating intelligence, sat at a crude table, poring over a sheaf of papers. Elara, her face pale and drawn, nervously fiddled with a collection of strange stones, her fingers tracing their jagged edges. Seraphina, her eyes closed, seemed lost in a world of her own making, a fragile aura surrounding her like a shimmering veil. And Marcus, his usually fiery presence subdued, stirred a pot over a small fire, his face etched with a weariness that hinted at suppressed power.

Thomas watched them from the shadows, a silent predator observing its prey. He felt no remorse, no hesitation. His mission was clear: capture or kill. Yet, even as he observed them, a flicker of something else stirred within him—a pang of... familiarity. It was a faint echo, a ghostly memory barely clinging to the edges of his consciousness, a sense of shared experience, of a past that had been violently ripped away.

He raised his hand, signaling for them to surrender. His enhanced vision pierced the gloom, allowing him to see the fear etched on their faces, the desperation in their eyes. Irina, ever the strategist, remained calm, her eyes locking with his in a silent battle of wills. Elara, ever vigilant, instinctively reached for one of her weather-shaping stones, her fingers tightening around its cold surface. Seraphina flinched, her senses picking up his intentions. Only Marcus seemed resigned, his gaze fixed on the flickering lamp, his hands hovering over the flames as if ready to unleash their destructive power.

"Come out," Thomas's voice echoed in the vast space, amplified by the building's acoustics. His voice was a low growl, devoid of emotion, a weapon as deadly as any firearm. "Your escape ends here."

Irina finally spoke, her voice a sharp counterpoint to his growl. "You think you can capture us, Thomas? You think you can control us like puppets?"

"I was created to do just that," he replied, his gaze unwavering. "And I will succeed."

"Created?" Elara's voice was barely a whisper, but Thomas heard every nuance, every tremor of doubt in her tone. The word hung in the air, heavy with unspoken history, with the weight of a shared past they were all desperately trying to forget.

The chase had begun, but it wasn't simply a hunter pursuing prey anymore. It was a confrontation with a past that refused to stay buried, a battle not only for survival but for the very essence of their being. The rain continued to fall outside, steady drumming against the roof, a reminder of the relentless march of time, of the unstoppable momentum of events that had led them to this desolate factory, to this fateful confrontation. The air crackled with unspoken tensions, with the raw energy of their unique powers, with the weight of their shared history, and with the chilling certainty that tonight, something would break. The hunt had begun, and it wouldn't end until someone was broken, someone was dead, or perhaps, something even more profound would be shattered: the carefully constructed facade of their individual realities.

The silence stretched, thick and suffocating, broken only by the rhythmic drip of water from a leaky pipe and the erratic beat of Thomas's own abnormally fast heart. He knew that the next move, the next sound, would determine the fate of them all. He was a weapon, yes, but he was also something more. He was a puzzle piece, a fragment of a twisted experiment that had irrevocably altered the course of history, leaving behind a trail of destruction and uncertainty that reached far beyond the walls of this abandoned factory. He was a hunter, but he was also hunted. By his past, by his own internal conflict, and by the undeniable truth that even the most rigorously trained soldier could not entirely control the unpredictable nature of human — or rather, superhuman – emotion. The game had begun, and the stakes were higher than he had ever imagined.

The flickering lamplight danced on Irina's face, highlighting the steely glint in her eyes. She signaled something to Elara, who, with a barely perceptible nod, reached for the stones again. The air around her began to crackle, the scent of ozone becoming increasingly sharp in Thomas's heightened senses. He knew what was coming: a weather manipulation spell, a storm to overwhelm him and provide them with a chance to escape. His instincts screamed at him to act, but a strange hesitation held him back, a lingering doubt rooted in the unsettling familiarity he felt towards these people, these hunted creatures, these… colleagues.

Marcus, too, was bracing himself, his aura shifting, the heat radiating from his body increasing, a subtle prelude to his pyrokinetic abilities. He was a volatile force, a walking inferno, but right now, he was strangely subdued, his fiery energy held in check. Seraphina, still with eyes closed, seemed to be sensing something, drawing in the ambient psychic energy, preparing for whatever confrontation was to come. The air in the cavernous space vibrated with unspoken power, a potent mixture of fear, defiance, and a strange, unsettling kinship.

Thomas moved, not with the cold efficiency of a trained assassin, but with a hesitant grace, a cautious step into the unknown. His heightened senses were overwhelming, the sounds smells, and sensations assaulting his awareness. He felt a connection to these people, a sense of being intertwined as if their fates were intricately linked by some unseen force. He was a weapon, yes, but he was also a pawn, a piece in a much larger game, a game orchestrated by the shadowy figures at Tempête, the scientists who had created them all and left them to fight their own battles in the decaying remnants of a forgotten world. He was a hunter, but tonight, he found himself questioning the very nature of his prey, the very purpose of his own existence, and the very essence of his loyalty. The game was far from over. In fact, it had just truly begun.

Irina's Resistance

The Parisian rain continued its relentless assault, but Irina, unlike Thomas, found little solace in its rhythmic drumming. She was holed up in a cramped attic room, the only light filtering through grimy skylights, illuminating dust motes dancing in the air like tiny, frantic spirits. The air hung thick with the scent of old paper, damp wood, and the ever-present metallic tang of fear. Her breath hitched in her chest; the sounds of Thomas's approach had been faint, almost imperceptible, but to her enhanced hearing, they were as clear as a gunshot. He was close.

Five years. Five years of running, five years of outsmarting the relentless machine that was Thomas, the weapon they had all become. But she knew this game couldn't last forever. Thomas's senses were acute, a honed predator's instinct guided by his enhanced abilities; it was only a matter of time before he cornered her. Her intelligence, the very thing that had kept her alive thus far, was now her greatest burden. She saw the intricate web of connections, the puppet masters pulling the strings from the shadows, and the terrifying scope of their ambition.

Irina wasn't merely evading Thomas; she was fighting a war against Tempete's legacy, against the very scientists who had permanently altered her existence. She had used her intellect to carve out a life in the shadows, a clandestine existence filled with coded messages, hidden identities, and constant vigilance. She had cultivated an elaborate network of contacts – disgruntled former Tempête associates, sympathetic journalists, and even corrupt officials – all crucial pieces in her complex game of survival.

Tonight, however, her resources felt thin. The attic was her last refuge, a temporary sanctuary tucked away in the labyrinthine heart of the city. She checked her meager supplies: a half-empty bottle of water, a stale baguette, and a worn copy of Baudelaire, a small comfort in her isolating reality. Her eyes, however, were fixed on a small, battered suitcase tucked beneath a pile of moth-eaten blankets. Inside lay her most valuable asset: her escape plan.

Irina's escape wasn't a matter of fleeing to some idyllic sanctuary. It was about dismantling the structure of her pursuers, unraveling the threads of the conspiracy that bound her and her fellow mutants. Her plan involved exploiting Tempete's internal conflicts and using their own hubris against them. She had gleaned information from her network, whispers of disagreements, of power struggles within the organization. There were those who regretted their creation, who yearned for a way to atone for their role in transforming humans into weapons. Irina intended to leverage this dissent.

Her intricate plan required precision, timing, and meticulous execution. She'd spent weeks meticulously arranging for forged documents, discreetly transferring funds, and establishing secret communication channels. It was a delicate dance, a high-stakes gamble, and one false step could cost her everything. The suitcase contained enough to secure her passage out of Paris, a forged passport, enough money to survive for a while, and a series of coded messages meant to initiate a chain reaction – exposing the darker side of Tempête and inciting a chain of events that might even lead to their downfall.

She ran a hand through her disheveled hair, the faint scent of lavender, her chosen disguise, clinging to her. The lavender wasn't just a scent; it was a carefully cultivated signal, a way to identify those she could trust amidst the city's treacherous underbelly. She'd learned to trust no one but herself, yet her survival depended on a delicate dance with those few who might be willing to assist her.

The floorboards creaked again, a sound that sent a jolt of adrenaline through her veins. This was it. She closed the suitcase with a decisive click, the sound a sharp contrast to the soft padding of Thomas's footsteps on the wooden stairs. Her mind raced, calculating probabilities, analyzing escape routes, anticipating Thomas's next move. She knew his tactics; he was methodical, precise, and a ruthless hunter. But she wasn't just prey; she was a strategist, a chess player who had spent years studying her opponent's every move.

She moved with the grace of a phantom, her body silent as she slipped through the shadows, away from the attic window, and into the dark recesses of the factory. The building was a maze of corridors, broken machinery, and crumbling walls. She had memorized the layout, using her exceptional memory to navigate the labyrinthine spaces.

The metallic tang of blood filled the air, sharper now, closer. Thomas was here.

Irina didn't run; she didn't panic. Instead, she utilized the shadows, the darkness itself becoming her weapon. She knew he relied on his enhanced senses, but his heightened perception could also be a disadvantage, overwhelming him in a space filled with conflicting stimuli. She employed a tactic she'd perfected over years of evasion: using the factory's chaotic environment against him, creating a symphony of sounds and smells to obscure her movements. She deliberately triggered a cascade of noises—a clatter of metal, the screech of rusted hinges, the drip, drip, drip of water echoing through the cavernous space. The factory became her orchestra, and each sounds a note in her cunning composition designed to disorient and delay him.

She moved through the factory like a wisp of smoke, her movements fluid, almost ethereal. She understood the psychology of her pursuer, the weight of the burden he carried, the internal conflict that tore at his loyalties. She knew that while he hunted her with lethal efficiency, part of him must also wrestle with the guilt of his actions.

She knew her time was short; every moment brought Thomas closer. She reached a heavily fortified section of the factory, a section she knew was heavily guarded by those who were fiercely loyal to Tempete's cause. This was a risk, a calculated gamble, but it was the only path to her escape. The section was a dead end, a trap for the unwary. But Irina wasn't unwary.

She slipped through a hidden passage, her knowledge of the factory's intricate structure her salvation. The air grew thick with the smell of chemicals, a familiar scent from her time at Tempête. This was the laboratory where the experiments that had altered their lives had taken place. It was dangerous territory, but it was also the key to her final gambit.

She reached a hidden alcove, revealing a secret passage leading to the city's underground tunnels, a network of forgotten pathways that crisscrossed beneath Paris. It was a labyrinthine escape route, one she'd discovered during her years of surveillance and infiltration.

Thomas's footsteps echoed closer, the relentless pursuit growing more urgent. She could hear his ragged breathing, the palpable frustration in his movements. He was close. Too close.

She heard his voice, a low growl of suppressed fury, cutting through the clamor of the factory. "Irina! I will find you!"

She paused a single breath before disappearing down the passage, leaving him to the echo of his own threats and his lingering doubt. The hunt was far from over, but for now, Irina had won a critical battle in this deadly game of cat and mouse. Her escape wasn't simply a flight; it was the first stage of a meticulously orchestrated plan to expose Tempête, to unravel the web of deceit that held them all captive, and to finally reclaim her stolen life. The true fight, the fight for her freedom, for the freedom of the others, was just beginning.

Elara's Weather Warfare

The Seine, usually a shimmering ribbon of silver threading through the heart of Paris, was now a raging, violent beast. Torrents of rain lashed against the ancient stones of the city, blurring the already indistinct gaslight glow into hazy halos. This was Elara's doing. She hadn't planned on such a dramatic display, but necessity, as they say, is the mother of invention. And Thomas, with his enhanced senses and relentless pursuit, was proving to be a particularly inventive adversary.

She'd been hiding in the catacombs, a labyrinthine network of tunnels beneath the city, a place both beautiful and terrifying in its cold, damp vastness. The air hung heavy with the scent of mildew and the ghosts of centuries past. The endless tunnels, stretching out into an echoing darkness, had offered a temporary sanctuary, but she knew it couldn't last. Thomas was methodical, relentless, a hound with a heightened sense of smell, tracking his prey with an almost supernatural precision.

Her escape from the military compound hadn't been elegant. It had been a desperate, chaotic scramble, a frantic dash through the rain-slicked streets, a whirlwind of panicked breaths and adrenaline-fueled sprints. But even then, as she'd felt his presence – that prickling sensation on the back of her neck, a premonition of his approach – she'd unleashed the first gust of wind, a swirling vortex that ripped through the courtyard, scattering guards and throwing their meticulously planned ambush into disarray.

That initial burst of power had been a gamble. She hadn't fully grasped the extent of her abilities, the sheer destructive force she could unleash. But the fear, the primal terror of capture, had unlocked something within her, a raw, untamed power that she was only beginning to understand. The rain that had followed had been a calculated choice, a deliberate obscuring of her tracks. The downpour wasn't just a natural phenomenon; it was a weapon, a carefully orchestrated curtain of water designed to mask her movements, to confound her pursuer's heightened senses.

Now, hunkered down in a forgotten alcove, the roar of the storm a deafening counterpoint to the frantic beat of her heart, she focused her energies. She could feel the city's pulse, the subterranean currents of water flowing beneath the cobblestones, the wind whipping through the narrow streets above. She was connected to it all, a conductor of the city's elemental symphony. She could feel Thomas approaching, his proximity a cold, chilling presence cutting through the storm's fury. He was close. Too close.

This was a different kind of fight; a battle fought not with fists or guns but with the very elements themselves. She could summon blizzards, torrential downpours, and even conjure miniature tornadoes. But such displays of power were risky. They were exhausting, leaving her vulnerable. She needed to conserve her energy and use her powers strategically to exploit the city's environment to her advantage.

Her plan was audacious, bordering on reckless, but it was her only chance. She would use the storm, the very chaos she'd unleashed, to create a diversion, a screen of confusion to mask her escape. She envisioned a series of localized weather events, small but strategically placed, a series of disruptive bursts of wind, pockets of intense rain, and temporary hailstorms, each designed to disorient Thomas and buy her precious seconds.

The first volley was a carefully aimed gust of wind that swept through a narrow alleyway, scattering debris and sending a shower of broken glass and loose tiles crashing to the ground. It was a sharp, piercing sound that cut through the roar of the storm, a sonic distraction amidst the conflict. Thomas, even with his enhanced hearing, would be momentarily disoriented, his focus broken, his pursuit momentarily thrown off course.

Then, she shifted her focus, drawing on the energy of the Seine, conjuring a sudden, intense burst of rain, creating a localized deluge that flooded a section of the street, turning it into a treacherous, impassable waterway. The water cascaded down the cobblestones, creating a wall of water that would momentarily halt Thomas's pursuit.

She moved further, her mind racing, her powers flowing, each targeted burst of wind, each downpour, each carefully aimed hailstone a calculated risk. She was playing a deadly game of cat and mouse, using the elements as her pawns, turning the city itself into a weapon. The Parisian streets became a treacherous battlefield, a landscape sculpted by her power, where the very elements themselves fought on her behalf.

But she knew that this couldn't last forever. Her powers, while potent, were finite. The strain was building, a pressure mounting in her chest, a throbbing headache threatening to overwhelm her. Each burst of energy drained her, leaving her weakened and vulnerable. She was pushing her limits, gambling with her own strength.

Thomas, however, was persistent. He was a shadow, a relentless force that seemed immune to the chaotic weather. Despite the downpour, despite the wind, despite the hail, he relentlessly pressed forward, a dark figure cutting through the storm, his pursuit undeterred.

As she moved through the twisting, turning labyrinth of Parisian streets, she felt the familiar prickling sensation on her skin, the sure sign of his proximity. He was close enough to taste the salt spray of the storm on his lips, close enough to feel the chilling bite of the wind.

She realized that she couldn't simply rely on the weather to escape; she needed to use the storm to her advantage in a more decisive way. She had to lure him into a trap. She needed to use the chaos, the fury of the storm, to conceal her movements. She would lead him on a chase, a dizzying, confusing pursuit, using the storm as a screen to obscure her true path, to mask her escape route.

It was a high-stakes gamble, but one she was willing to take. It was either that or face capture and an unknown, probably grim fate. She'd seen the effects of the military's experiments on the others; she wasn't willing to become another subject in their cruel experiments.

She focused her powers, channeling her energy into a larger, more complex weather pattern. The storm intensified, its fury escalating to a frightening level. The rain fell in sheets, blinding and deafening. The wind howled like a banshee; the air itself charged with electrical energy. It was magnificent and terrifying.

She channeled her strength, carefully weaving a path through the storm, weaving it into a maze of rain, wind, and lightning. She felt a growing exhaustion, the relentless strain pushing her to the very brink of her abilities. But the image of Thomas's relentless pursuit spurred her on. Freedom was within her grasp, a tantalizing yet elusive prize.

As she weaved through the storm-lashed streets, she could almost feel the rage of Thomas, his frustrated pursuit. She had him disoriented, and he was searching for her in the wrong place. She had gained the upper hand, but only for a brief moment. She knew that once the storm subsided, he would pick up her trail once again. This was a temporary victory; the war was far from over.

The escape route was harrowing, a desperate dash through the heart of the storm, but as she emerged from the storm's embrace, she found herself at the edge of the city, standing under the pale glow of the early morning dawn. The rain had subsided, the wind had died down, and the city looked shaken but unscathed. The hunt was far from over; it was merely another chapter in a long, dangerous game. But for now, Elara had won a crucial battle, a hard-fought victory in this deadly game of cat and mouse. And the city, witness to her weather-warfare, held its breath.

Seraphina's Psychic Defense

The chill of the Parisian dawn clung to Seraphina like a shroud. Elara's storm had subsided, leaving behind a city slick with rain and heavy with the scent of wet cobblestones and fear. Seraphina, her breath misting in the cold air, huddled deeper into the alleyway, the shadows offering a meager respite from Thomas's relentless pursuit. He was close. She could feel it, a prickling unease at the edges of her consciousness, a faint tremor in the psychic landscape. It wasn't a precise location but more a pervasive sense of his proximity, a predator circling its prey.

Her escape from the military compound had been a blur of frantic movement and sheer terror. The enhanced senses of Thomas would have made the slightest sound a beacon, a siren's call to his deadly pursuit. She had relied on instinct, a gut feeling honed by years of living under the shadow of fear. She had slipped through the gaps in the security, a phantom flitting through the darkened corridors, her heart hammering against her ribs like a trapped bird.

But now, the adrenaline had faded, leaving behind a gnawing exhaustion and a bone-deep dread. She needed to think, to plan, to use her gift to its fullest potential. Her telepathy wasn't just about reading minds; it was a complex interplay of emotions, intentions, and subconscious whispers. She could sense the fear of the city, a low hum of anxiety that vibrated through the very stones beneath her feet. But more importantly, she could attempt to penetrate the psychic shield Thomas had erected around himself.

She closed her eyes, focusing her mind, letting her consciousness ripple outwards like waves across a still pond. It was a delicate dance, a careful probing, a search for the faintest echo of Thomas's presence. She felt the city's fear, the rhythmic pulse of thousands of hearts beating in unison, background noise to the sharper, more insistent rhythm of Thomas's thoughts.

He was methodical, relentless, a machine programmed for destruction. His thoughts were sharp, precise, devoid of emotion

– or so it seemed at first. Beneath the surface of his cold, calculated strategy, she detected a flicker of something else, a faint tremor of doubt, a whisper of regret. It was barely perceptible, a fleeting shadow in the depths of his mind, but it was there. A crack in the meticulously constructed façade of the perfect killing machine.

This crack, however small, was a foothold. Seraphina reached out, her consciousness probing the edges of his psychic fortress, seeking weaknesses. She delved into the memories he tried to suppress, the echoes of his training, and the faces of his former comrades. The faces of her friends.

She saw flashes of the laboratory, the cold steel tables, the scientists in their white coats, their faces blurred by the passage of time, but their cold, detached ambition crystal clear. She saw Dmitri's raw power, the way his strength bent metal and shattered stone. She saw Irina's brilliant mind, her intellect a whirlwind of complex equations and strategic maneuvers. And then, she saw herself, caught in a cage of fear, her desperate attempts to escape.

Thomas's memories were fragmented, scattered like shards of glass. He had undergone an extensive memory alteration, but the wounds remained, buried deep but not entirely obliterated. Seraphina sensed the lingering pain, the guilt, the torment of a man forced to betray his own humanity.

His next move, she discovered, was audacious but predictable. He was using a network of informants – former members of the Tempête organization who had been blackmailed into submission. These informants were spread throughout Paris, their collective consciousness forming a rudimentary network of spies, subtly reporting her movements to Thomas. The network was loosely organized, but its effect was devastating.

She needed to disrupt this network, to blind Thomas, to buy herself some time. She couldn't directly confront him, not yet. He was too strong, too fast, too well-trained. Instead, she would use his own tools against him.

She reached out, her telepathy weaving a subtle web of deception. She planted false information into the minds of his informants, misleading them and creating chaos and confusion in their ranks. She didn't erase their memories; she simply altered their perceptions, painting a distorted picture of her whereabouts. She sent them racing on wild goose chases, leading them through winding streets and hidden alleyways while she slipped away undetected.

It was a risky gamble, akin to walking a tightrope across a chasm. One wrong move, one slip in concentration, and Thomas could sense the manipulation, exposing her. But the risk was worth taking. The faint tremor of doubt she had felt in Thomas's mind gave her hope. Perhaps the machine wasn't as perfect as they had made it seem.

As she moved through the city, her mind weaving a tapestry of illusions and misdirection, Seraphina noticed something else: a subtle shift in the psychic landscape. It was faint, almost imperceptible, but she sensed a new presence, an outsider, someone who was not part of the hunt. This person was observing her, watching from the shadows, their consciousness cloaked in a veil of secrecy. But Seraphina felt a flicker of curiosity, not malice, emanating from this unknown observer.

The unknown watcher was not an enemy but a mystery. It was another piece of the puzzle, a potential ally or perhaps just a witness to the deadly game unfolding in the shadows of Paris. But for now, Seraphina focused on her immediate goal: to stay alive. The hunt was far from over. It was merely a new stage in a long, dangerous game, and she was determined to play it to the bitter end.

The rain had stopped, but the city still felt cold, damp, and heavy with unspoken fears. Each shadow held the potential for Thomas, a predator always lurking just beyond sight, a constant threat hanging in the air like a poisonous fog. Seraphina knew she couldn't outrun him forever. She had to find a way to fight back, to turn the tables on her pursuer.

Her escape route led her through a labyrinthine network of backstreets and hidden courtyards, and each turn a gamble, each shadow a potential hiding place for her relentless hunter. She moved with the grace of a phantom, her steps silent, her movements fluid, a ghost flitting through the city's underbelly. Her telepathy was her shield, her sword, her guide.

Using her powers, she subtly influenced the thoughts of those she passed, planting suggestions, creating distractions, and weaving a hypnotic web of misdirection. Shopkeepers saw customers where there were none, hurrying passersby, veering away from her path, avoiding eye contact. It was a constant, draining process, but it bought her precious time and space to plan her next move.

She knew she couldn't rely solely on deception. She needed a more strategic approach. She needed to understand Thomas's thought processes, his patterns, and his weaknesses. She needed to delve deeper into his fractured memories, to unravel the mysteries of his past, and to understand the lingering echoes of his humanity.

Her investigation into Thomas's past led her to an abandoned section of the city, where the dilapidated buildings stood as silent witnesses to forgotten stories. She entered a derelict building, its decaying walls whispering tales of a bygone era. As she moved deeper into the building, she felt a wave of psychic energy, a strong presence that resonated with Thomas's past.

The presence led her to a dusty room, where she found a collection of old photographs and personal letters scattered on a crumbling table. The pictures were blurry and faded, but Seraphina recognized the faces – the scientists of Tempête and, most importantly, a younger Thomas, his eyes reflecting a blend of hope and apprehension. The letters were filled with personal confessions, the anxieties and dreams of a man struggling to reconcile his scientific ambitions with his own conscience.

The documents revealed a deeper layer of Thomas's story, showing not only his rigorous training and conditioning but also his internal struggles, his repressed emotions, and his yearning for connection and belonging. This was evidence of the humanity that lay buried beneath the layers of training and conditioning. This was the key to understanding Thomas, the key to unlocking his potential for redemption. The hunt had become something more than a mere pursuit of survival; it was a journey into the depths of human nature, a confrontation with the consequences of scientific ambition and the human cost of unchecked power. It was the first step towards finding a way to break through the ice wall that had separated them, to help Thomas find his way back from the darkness.

Marcus's Pyrokinetic Challenges

The biting wind whipped through the narrow alleyways of Marseille, carrying with it the scent of salt and decay. Marcus hunched deeper into the shadows, his breath misting in the frigid air. He clutched the worn leather satchel containing his meager possessions – a few francs, a change of clothes, and a well-thumbed copy of Baudelaire's *Les Fleurs du Mal*. The poems, filled with darkness and despair, strangely mirrored his own internal state. He was a creature of fire, a living paradox, consumed by the very element he struggled to control.

His pyrokinesis, a gift and a curse, was a constant, simmering threat. The slightest surge of anger, fear, or even exhilaration sent jolts of heat coursing through him, igniting the air around him with barely suppressed flames. He'd learned to control it, somewhat, through years of rigorous self-discipline and meditation – techniques gleaned from stolen monastic texts and whispered conversations with street urchins who'd witnessed his outbursts. But control was a fragile thing, a dam constantly threatened by the rising tide of his inner turmoil.

He'd been lucky so far. He'd managed to avoid Thomas's relentless pursuit for five years, living on the fringes of society, a ghost in the bustling port city. He'd found work as a dockhand, his strength surprisingly useful in the grueling labor, but the proximity to the flammable materials was a constant, gnawing anxiety. He'd seen the damage his uncontrolled power could inflict; he'd accidentally set fire to a stack of crates once, nearly destroying the entire dock. The memory still haunted him, a stark reminder of his volatile nature.

He knew Thomas was hunting him. He felt it, not with the clarity of Seraphina's telepathy, but as a low, persistent hum in the background of his existence, a premonition of danger that clung to him like the city's ever-present humidity. The whispers in the taverns, the wary glances from the dockworkers – all hinted at Thomas's presence, a shadow lurking just beyond the periphery of his vision.

Tonight, the hum was louder, closer.

He shifted his weight, a spark of unintended energy flickering around his fingertips. He quickly grounded himself, focusing on his breathing, forcing the flames back into the recesses of his being. The meditative exercises were his only defense against the unpredictable nature of his powers. He needed to find a new hiding place, something more secure, more secluded than this decaying alleyway. The constant movement the endless fear of discovery, was draining him, both physically and mentally.

He thought of the abandoned catacombs that snaked beneath the city, a labyrinthine network of tunnels and chambers rumored to be the resting place of forgotten saints and forgotten secrets. They would offer the perfect sanctuary, a place where he could disappear into the shadows, unburdened by the fear of detection.

But the catacombs were also a dangerous place, a maze of twisting passages where a single wrong turn could lead to utter disorientation and certain death. And even within their protective darkness, he couldn't entirely escape the threat of Thomas. The man's enhanced senses, honed to perfection through years of rigorous military training, would make him a difficult adversary to evade even in the most impenetrable of lairs.

The prospect of the catacombs filled him with a strange mix of fear and exhilaration. Fear of the unknown, fear of Thomas, and fear of his own power. Exhilaration at the thought of finally finding a place where he could truly hide, a place where he wouldn't have to constantly watch over his shoulder, a place where the flames within him wouldn't be a constant threat.

He began walking, his footsteps echoing in the empty alleyway. The wind picked up, carrying with it the distant sound of church bells, their mournful chimes a somber counterpoint to the thrumming anxiety in his chest. The city, usually vibrant and alive, felt cold and hostile, a testament to the danger that perpetually shadowed him.

As he ventured towards the outskirts of the city, the urban sprawl gave way to crumbling stone walls and overgrown vegetation. He could feel the earth beneath his feet shifting, becoming softer and damp, a subtle indication that he was nearing the entrance to the catacombs.

The entrance was hidden behind a thicket of thorny bushes, barely visible in the twilight. He pushed aside the branches, careful not to make a sound, and peered into the darkness. A damp chill enveloped him, the air thick with the scent of mildew and earth. He hesitated, his hand instinctively reaching for his satchel, his fingers brushing against the worn leather.

The decision was made. He couldn't stay here, hidden in plain sight, constantly burdened by the fear of discovery. He needed the catacombs, the labyrinthine security they offered, the solace of darkness. This was a gamble, a dangerous one, but it was the only chance he had.

He stepped into the darkness, the cool, damp air a stark contrast to the chilling wind that had pursued him through the city. He pulled out a small oil lamp from his satchel, striking a flint and steel to ignite the wick. The small flame cast long, dancing shadows on the walls, turning the familiar fear into something more tangible, less abstract. It was a familiar fear, and in a strange way, it was comforting.

He moved deeper into the catacombs, the rhythmic drip of water echoing in the stillness. He navigated the narrow passages, his heart pounding in his chest, each turn revealing a new chamber, a new possibility. This wasn't merely escape; it was a plunge into the unknown, a desperate attempt to outmaneuver his relentless pursuer. He imagined Thomas, his enhanced senses piercing the darkness, his heightened intellect mapping out the catacombs just as he was. The game of cat and mouse continued, now beneath the city, in this claustrophobic realm of shadow and bone.

He moved with the agility of a hunted animal, his senses heightened, his pyrokinesis held in check, a potential weapon that could as easily become his downfall. He had to be cautious, mindful of every step, every breath, every flicker of his latent power. One slip, one uncontrolled burst of flame, and the catacombs would become his tomb.

The hunt had entered a new phase, a descent into a subterranean world, a descent into the depths of his own being. The fight for survival wasn't just against Thomas; it was against himself, against the volatile power that threatened to consume him. The Parisian rain the urban clamor, was replaced by the dripping water and the oppressive silence of the ancient catacombs. In the heart of this subterranean labyrinth, Marcus's struggle for survival was no longer a chase but a desperate battle against his own inner demons. The flickering lamplight only illuminated the immediate path ahead, leaving the vast majority of his existence in an unforgiving darkness. The darkness of the catacombs mirrored the darkness within him, the relentless threat of his own power. The hunt had begun anew, beneath the city, in the heart of fear and uncertainty. And in the heart of the catacombs, Marcus knew the game was far from over.

Chapter 4: Fractured Loyalties

The Scientists Dilemma

The air in the dilapidated laboratory hung thick with the scent of ozone and stale coffee, a stark contrast to the sterile, clinical atmosphere that had once reigned supreme. Dust motes danced in the weak beams of light filtering through the grimy windows, illuminating the weary faces of the remaining members of Tempête. Dr. Dubois, his usually immaculate lab coat stained and rumpled, paced restlessly, his agitation a palpable presence in the room. Dr. Moreau, ever the pragmatist, sat hunched over a complex array of instruments, his brow furrowed in concentration, while Dr. Petrova, her normally sharp gaze clouded with uncertainty, stared blankly at the swirling chemicals in a beaker. Only Dr. Thorne, his usual jovial demeanor replaced with a grim determination, remained relatively still, his hands clasped tightly in his lap.

The success of their project, the creation of enhanced individuals, had been a double-edged sword, a triumph-stained crimson with the blood of ethical compromises. The military's intervention had stripped them of their autonomy, transforming their noble quest for a cure into a macabre experiment in human augmentation. The escape of the mutants, the subsequent hunt orchestrated by Thomas, and the devastating consequences that followed had left them reeling, their faith in their own work shattered.

"This... this serum," Dubois stammered, his voice barely above a whisper, gesturing towards a flask containing a shimmering, opalescent liquid. "It's our only chance. Our only way to... to escape this."

The memory-erasing serum, a byproduct of their failed attempts to replicate Thomas's enhancements, offered a grim solution to their predicament. It was a chance to forget, to erase the horrors they had witnessed, the moral compromises they had made, the lives they had irrevocably altered. But it was also a betrayal, a surrender of their creation, a cowardly abandonment of the very project that had consumed their lives.

Moreau, ever the voice of reason, spoke cautiously, "Are we sure this is the right course of action? To simply… erase ourselves from this?"

Petrova's voice, laced with exhaustion and regret, chimed in, "What choice do we have, Antoine? The military will never let us go. They'll continue to exploit our work, regardless of the cost. This… this is the only way to stop them."

Thorne, his voice heavy with the weight of unspoken guilt, nodded slowly. "We've created a monster, Moreau. A monster we can no longer control. Perhaps… perhaps oblivion is the only merciful escape."

But even as they discussed their desperate plan, a dissonant note echoed in their deliberations. Dr. Reed, his face etched with a chilling determination, remained silent, his eyes fixed on the serum with an unsettling intensity. He had witnessed the brutal training, the callous disregard for human life, and the transformation of their hopeful endeavor into a horrifying tool of war. Yet, unlike his colleagues, he saw not failure but potential. He saw not a reason to erase but a reason to continue.

Reed's faith in their work, his unwavering belief in the potential of their enhancements, seemed to him a beacon in the encroaching darkness. He believed that their discoveries, while misused, held the key to a future where humanity transcended its physical limitations, where illness and weakness were mere relics of a bygone era. The escape of the mutants, the military's pursuit, the ethical dilemmas – these were mere setbacks, temporary obstacles in the path towards a greater destiny.

The others sensed his dissent, the unspoken chasm that separated him from their despair. Dubois, his voice trembling, confronted him, "Reed, you cannot be serious. You saw what they did, the way they used those children. How can you still believe in this?"

Reed's eyes were cold, devoid of the usual warmth and enthusiasm that had once characterized him. "You focus on the immediate consequences, on the present horrors. But I see the future, Dubois. I see a world beyond disease, beyond weakness, beyond the limitations of our frail humanity. This is not about them, Dubois. It is about us, about our potential, about the future of humankind."

He looked at the serum with a chilling indifference, his words laced with an almost disturbing conviction. "Your amnesia will be your shield, your refuge. But my memory? It will be my weapon. It will be my guide to the future that awaits us. A future you are too cowardly to face."

The argument raged on, the room filled with the clash of their convictions, their differing interpretations of morality and scientific advancement. Each scientist, trapped in their own labyrinth of guilt and ambition, wrestled with their conscience. The air thrummed with the weight of their decision, the potential consequences of choosing oblivion over responsibility. The memory serum represented not merely an escape from their past but a profound choice concerning their future, their legacy, and the future of humankind. It was a choice that would determine not only their own fate but the trajectory of science itself.

The silence that descended once they had all agreed to take the serum was heavy with foreboding. They were not erasing their memories to escape punishment or shame; they were erasing them to protect the world from a danger they had unwittingly unleashed. It was a desperate act of self-preservation, but it was also an act of profound irresponsibility, a shirking of their duties as scientists and as human beings. Their hands trembled as they each drank the serum, the opalescent liquid promising oblivion but also promising a chilling potential: that the monstrous project of Tempête would continue, driven by a single, unwavering mind untouched by doubt or regret. The decision to erase their memories would become a testament to their own fractured loyalties – loyalties that had been splintered by the conflicting demands of ambition, duty, and conscience. The memory serum would grant them temporary peace, but it would also sow the seeds of a future more uncertain and perilous than any they had ever imagined. The future, like their fractured loyalties, hung precariously in the balance, waiting for the inevitable next chapter to unfold. The weight of their collective amnesia would fall, eventually, upon the unsuspecting world. The seeds of Tempête had been sown, and they were far from dormant.

Reeds Unwavering Belief

The others had left, their minds wiped clean, their consciences absolved by a treacherous chemical concoction. They had fled the wreckage of their ambition, leaving behind the ghost of Tempête, a chilling monument to their hubris. But Dr. Reed remained. He stood amidst the scattered equipment, the faint scent of burnt chemicals clinging to the air like a shroud. The silence in the laboratory was profound, broken only by the occasional drip of water from a leaky pipe, each drop echoing the slow, deliberate rhythm of his own heartbeat. He didn't flinch at the desolation; he saw not ruin but potential.

His gaze lingered on the half-finished notes scattered across his workbench, scrawled equations and diagrams hinting at the unfinished chapters of their research. He touched the brittle paper, his fingers tracing the faded ink. These weren't just equations; they were the blueprints for a new world, a world where disease bowed to the will of science, where humanity transcended its frail limitations. The serum, the escape of his colleagues—these were mere setbacks, temporary inconveniences in the grand scheme of his vision. He saw the fear in their eyes, the guilt that gnawed at their consciences, but he saw none of that in himself. He saw only the unwavering possibility, the tantalizing glimpse of a future shaped by their relentless pursuit of power.

Reed wasn't a monster, at least not in his own eyes. He believed, with a conviction that bordered on religious zeal, in the sanctity of his work. He didn't see the mutants as weapons; he saw them as advancements, as the next step in human evolution. The military's brutal methods and their callous disregard for the human cost that was a perversion of his vision. He had always intended to use the power of Tempête for the greater good, to eradicate diseases that had plagued humanity for centuries. He had envisioned a world free from suffering, a world where his creations would be saviors, not soldiers. The reality, however, had been a twisted mockery of his noble intentions.

The memory serum, he admitted to himself, was a regrettable necessity. It was a way to protect their work, to shield it from the prying eyes of those who would exploit it for their own nefarious purposes. He had never considered the ethical implications of wiping their minds, not truly. The immediate need to preserve his research had eclipsed any pangs of conscience. His focus, always razor-sharp, was trained solely on the pursuit of scientific advancement, a relentless drive that blurred the lines between ambition and obsession.

He began to meticulously clean the lab, carefully storing away the remaining materials. Each vial, each instrument held a piece of the puzzle, a fragment of his life's work. He moved with deliberate precision, his actions reflecting a mind untouched by doubt, a soul immune to remorse. He wasn't blind to the potential consequences; he knew the power they had unleashed was both magnificent and terrifying. But he believed he could control it, that he could steer it towards a benevolent future. He considered himself a shepherd guiding a flock of powerful, volatile sheep, and he would not allow fear or guilt to deter him.

As he worked, his thoughts drifted back to Dmitri, the first success of Tempête. He remembered the boy's hesitant steps, his tentative exploration of his newly found strength. He had seen the fear in his eyes at first, the confusion and terror of an altered reality. But Dmitri had adapted. He had learned to control his power. This adaptability, this innate capacity for growth, was the essence of what Reed saw as potential, the very justification for their work.

His mind traced the arc of each subsequent mutant: Irina's extraordinary intellect, which, in Reed's eyes, was a gift of unparalleled potential; Thomas's almost supernatural senses, the perfect instrument for precision and healing; Elara's mastery over the elements, a testament to the boundless capacity for human evolution. Each individual, he argued, was a masterpiece, a product of scientific ingenuity and unwavering dedication. The brutality inflicted upon them by the military was a separate issue, a regrettable obstacle in the path of his grand vision.

The thought of Thomas, his former colleague turned relentless hunter, briefly flickered in his mind. He did not feel guilt or remorse; he felt only a tinge of disappointment. Thomas had been their most successful creation, a perfect embodiment of the enhanced human form. But he had failed to realize his full potential, allowing his training to warp his sense of loyalty, twisting his innate goodness into a ruthless efficiency. To Reed, Thomas's actions were a failure of the training, not a failure of the science.

Reed's unwavering belief wasn't based on ignorance. He understood the risks, the moral ambiguities, and the potential for catastrophic consequences. He'd seen the fear in his colleagues' eyes, the haunting realization of the monster they had created. But he held onto his vision with stubborn tenacity. He believed that the benefits far outweighed the risks, that the cure for consumption, the eradication of disease, and the very possibility of improving the human condition justified the cost.

The memory serum, he reasoned, was not an act of cowardice but an act of practicality. His colleagues were emotionally burdened and psychologically shattered by the weight of their creation. Their fears their doubts would only hinder the progress of their research. He saw himself as the guardian, the protector of their legacy. He wouldn't let their hesitation, their moral misgivings, derail the project. The world, he believed, needed what they had created. The potential benefits were too immense to abandon.

He spent days and weeks poring over the data, refining the formulas, and meticulously reconstructing the experiments. He worked tirelessly, fueled by a powerful conviction and a single-minded determination to continue where they had left off. The empty space where his colleagues once stood became a symbolic void – a representation of the fragility of human conscience compared to the ironclad certainty of scientific pursuit.

He started to improve the serum, refining it, making it more potent and more effective. He wasn't just erasing memories; he was shaping the future, meticulously crafting a narrative that would allow his vision to take hold. The world, in his mind, deserved a chance at a better tomorrow, even if it meant some sacrifices along the way. Those sacrifices, he reasoned, were merely stepping stones towards a grander, more magnificent future. The potential benefits outweighed the cost; in his eyes, the end justified the means. And so, Dr. Reed, alone in the ruins of Tempête, stood as a testament to the unwavering belief of one man, a belief that could change the world or, perhaps, destroy it. His legacy, etched in the methods and the forgotten memories, was set to unfold, a silent promise of a future fraught with both hope and dread. The consequences of his actions remained unseen, a grim testament to the seductive power of unchecked ambition and the potentially devastating consequences of a faith untainted by doubt. The future hung precariously in the balance, waiting for the next chapter to begin.

The Memory Serum

The serum shimmered in the test tube, a viscous, opalescent liquid that held the potential for both salvation and damnation. Dr. Reed, his face etched with the weariness of countless sleepless nights, examined it with a clinical detachment that belied the turmoil within. He had refined the formula, stripping away impurities and enhancing its potency. It was no longer a crude concoction, a hasty byproduct of a failed experiment; it was a weapon, a tool for sculpting reality itself. The initial duplications had been flawed, leaving behind fragmented memories of ghost-like echoes of the past that haunted their subjects. But this—this was different. This was a clean, efficient, complete erasure.

He swirled the serum gently, the light catching the iridescent particles suspended within. He thought of Dubois, Moreau, Petrova, Thorne—their faces, once sharp with ambition and driven by scientific fervor, now vacant, replaced with the placid, almost vacant expressions of the memory-erased. He had offered them the serum, a bitter solace for the horrors they had witnessed, the choices they had made. They had accepted, gladly, escaping the weight of their guilt, the crushing burden of their knowledge. He, however, carried that burden alone.

The ethical implications pressed upon him, a suffocating weight that he constantly tried to ignore. He justified his actions, weaving elaborate mental justifications to appease his conscience. The serum, he argued, was not about obliterating history; it was about rewriting it, about creating a future free from the mistakes of the past, a future where the horrors of Tempête could be relegated to myth, a forgotten nightmare. He envisioned a world where the knowledge gained, the power harnessed, could be used for good, unburdened by the ethical baggage of its origins. The very existence of the enhanced individuals, the mutants, he reasoned, was a testament to the potential of his work.

But the faces of his former colleagues continued to haunt him. He saw the fleeting moments of recognition before the serum's effects took hold. They were terrified. Not of the serum itself but of the implications of its use, of the potential for its misuse. Their fear had mirrored his own, yet he had persevered, convinced his vision justified the means. He had taken it upon himself to play God, to erase the past and shape the future according to his own design.

He picked up a worn notebook, its pages filled with equations and scrawled notes. He'd meticulously documented every step of the serum's development, charting its progression from a flawed, unpredictable substance to the refined instrument it had become. The margins were filled with philosophical musings and ethical dilemmas wrestled with and ultimately dismissed. The weight of his ambition was profound, a suffocating pressure that threatened to crush him.

He spent days, weeks, sometimes months refining the formula, testing and retesting, meticulously documenting each experiment. He performed countless trials on animals first—dogs, cats, rabbits. He observed the effects, recording behavioral changes, physiological responses, and the lingering traces of fragmented memory. Each successful animal trial brought him closer to his goal, yet each success also deepened his internal conflict. He was walking a tightrope, balancing the potential for good against undeniable ethical transgressions.

He understood the inherent risks. What if the serum caused unforeseen neurological damage? What if, in erasing the past, it also obliterated essential parts of the self, leaving the recipients empty husks, devoid of identity? The possibility chilled him, yet the allure of a better future, a future cleansed of the past's mistakes, held an irresistible appeal. He had seen firsthand the devastating power the Tempête mutants could wield. Their enhanced abilities, though extraordinary, had been a weapon in the wrong hands, capable of incredible destruction. Eradicating the memory of Tempête itself, he believed, could mitigate this danger.

The irony wasn't lost on him. He was using science to erase science, to bury the past under a veil of manufactured forgetfulness. He was creating a new reality, a carefully constructed illusion where the horrors of Tempête never existed. But at what cost? He had condemned his former colleagues to a life of manufactured oblivion, of stolen identities. Had he, in his ambition to create a better future, condemned them to a worse fate?

The weight of his decision pressed down on him, the guilt gnawing at his conscience. The quiet hum of the laboratory equipment was a constant reminder of his isolation, his solitude in the face of his monumental undertaking. Yet, he could not turn back. He had gone too far. The serum represented years of work, the culmination of his life's ambition. His belief in its potential, in its ability to create a better world, had become an unshakeable faith impervious to doubt. The potential benefits outweighed any cost. The end, he told himself, justified the means.

He continued his work, driven by a fierce determination. He meticulously documented the serum's properties, its effects, and its potential applications. He expanded his research, exploring ways to refine it further to make it even more potent and more precise. He began to experiment with memory implantation, attempting to replace the erased memories with carefully constructed narratives, shaping the identities of his subjects according to his design.

He was no longer just erasing the past; he was creating it. He was rewriting history, shaping the future, and forging a new reality according to his own vision. As he delved deeper into his work, the ethical considerations and the moral dilemmas faded into the background, overshadowed by his unwavering belief in the righteousness of his cause. He was creating a new dawn, a future free from the shadows of Tempête, a future where his creation, the memory-erasing serum, would be the key to a better tomorrow. But even as he felt the thrill of his accomplishment, a cold dread crept into his heart. He had erased the past, but the future remained uncertain, a terrifying expanse of unknown consequences waiting to unfold. His legacy, a double-edged sword of progress and oblivion, hung precariously in the balance. The question that remained unanswered, the one that haunted his every waking moment, was whether his actions would lead to salvation or damnation. He alone bore the weight of that answer, and he could only wait and watch as his creation unfurled its consequences, for better or for worse, upon the world. His success had brought about a terrible quiet, the silent aftermath of a storm of his own making.

Reed's Defiance

He stood alone amidst the gleaming steel and glass, the remnants of their ambitious and ultimately terrifying project. The air, thick with the scent of antiseptic and the faint, metallic tang of blood from countless experiments, felt different now, lighter somehow, yet heavier with the weight of his own unwavering resolve.

He hadn't shared their qualms, their gnawing guilt. He saw the memory-erasing serum not as a shameful escape, but as a necessary precaution, a regrettable but ultimately justifiable measure to protect their creation, their work. They had stumbled upon something extraordinary, something that could reshape the very fabric of human potential. To abandon it now, to erase the very memory of their triumph and their failures, felt to him like a betrayal of science itself. Their fears, their ethical anxieties, were a luxury he couldn't afford. He had seen the potential, the breathtaking possibilities, and he would not let it be extinguished.

His colleagues, blinded by remorse, had focused only on the ethical implications, the monstrous potential for misuse. He understood their concerns, of course, but he saw beyond the immediate horrors. He envisioned a world where disease was eradicated, where human limitations were transcended, a world where humanity's potential was amplified a thousandfold. He saw the possibility of a brighter future built upon the foundation of their groundbreaking work. He saw beyond the ethical quagmire and into a potential utopia.

He walked to the nearest workbench, his gaze drifting over the meticulously organized instruments, each with its own story of success and failure. The abandoned syringes, still bearing traces of the serum, seemed to mock him, a testament to the cowardice of his departing companions. He scoffed at their fear. Fear was a luxury he couldn't afford. He had a responsibility, a mission, that transcended personal anxieties. He had to continue.

The project, codenamed "Phoenix," had been their obsession for over a decade. The creation of enhanced individuals, mutants gifted with extraordinary abilities, had been fraught with peril and countless failures. Yet, their successes were undeniable. Dmitri, the first, possessed inhuman strength and the ability to heal from almost any injury. Irina's intellect surpassed that of any human being alive. Thomas, with his enhanced senses and unparalleled healing abilities, had been their ultimate creation—a weapon, a tool, now seemingly lost to them. Elara, Seraphina, and Marcus—each possessed their unique gifts, each a testament to the boundless potential of human genetic manipulation.

But the military's intervention, the brutal training they subjected the enhanced individuals to, had poisoned the project. Their dream of a brighter future had been twisted into a nightmare of weaponization. The escape of the enhanced individuals, their transformation into fugitives hunted by their own creation—Thomas—had cast a long, dark shadow over their work. Yet, Reed saw none of this as a failure. It was merely a setback, a temporary obstacle on the path to progress.

He began reviewing the data, his fingers flying across the keyboard. The countless hours spent analyzing genetic sequences, meticulously charting physiological changes, the countless trials and errors—they were all recorded in the vast databases. He delved back into the research that had led to the memory-erasing serum, scrutinizing the formulas and analyzing the potential side effects. The serum, while effective, was crude and imperfect. He needed to refine it to create a more potent, more predictable version. He would develop better control over the process and eliminate the unpredictable side effects.

The escape of the enhanced individuals their transformation into targets, fueled his determination. He wasn't driven by ambition, not in the usual sense. He wasn't seeking fame or fortune. He was driven by a cold, clinical objectivity, a belief in the inherent potential of his work. He saw the chaos caused by their uncontrolled creations, the suffering they had unintentionally inflicted, not as a disapproval of their work but as evidence of its unfinished nature.

He worked tirelessly, day and night, fueled by coffee and sheer willpower. He redesigned experimental protocols, adjusted variables, refining his techniques. He revisited the notes from the failed attempts at replicating Thomas's abilities. Each failure was a lesson learned, a step forward toward a better understanding. He was building upon the ruins of the past, but he was building.

He had to refine the enhancement process, making it more predictable and more controllable. He had to eliminate the unpredictable mutations and the dangerous side effects. He had to create individuals with specific, controlled abilities, individuals who wouldn't be prone to spontaneous outbursts of power or unpredictable behavior. He had to make them controllable. He needed to perfect the process to create not just enhanced individuals but enhanced soldiers, enhanced allies, and enhanced humanity. And he would. He had to.

He was aware of the inherent dangers and the ethical pitfalls. The possibility of misuse the potential for catastrophic consequences, weighed heavily on him. He wasn't blind to the moral complexities of his undertaking. But he believed in the inherent good, the boundless potential of his work. He believed he could harness this power, control it, and use it for the benefit of mankind.

The weight of the world rested on his shoulders. The potential for good and evil, both, were his burden to carry. He knew his colleagues would condemn him would view him as a reckless fanatic, blinded by ambition. They would see him as a monster, a creator of monsters. But he didn't care. He was driven by something beyond mere ambition. He was driven by a vision of faith in the potential of his creation. A faith that would allow him to overcome the shadow of his past and forge a brighter future. The world, after all, was on the brink of unimaginable changes. The next world war was looming, the darkness threatened to engulf the world. Perhaps, just perhaps, the monstrous tools he created could be humanity's last hope. He had to perfect them, perfect his vision before it was too late.

Months turned into years. The laboratory, once a place of shared ambition and collaboration, became his solitary sanctuary, a testament to his unwavering commitment. The silence, once a burden, became his companion, the hum of machinery his lullaby. He was alone in his endeavor, but he was not afraid. He had his work, his vision, and that was enough. He would succeed. He had to. The future, the fate of humanity, depended on it. He would not fail. Not now. Not ever. The ethical implications and the potential for catastrophe were all secondary to his singular purpose. He had to continue, for the future of humankind hung in the balance. And he was the only one left who could see it. He was the only one left who could save it. The world, after all, needed heroes, and sometimes, heroes are forged in the fires of moral ambiguity.

Chapter 5: Years Of Pursuit

Five Years of Hunting

The Parisian rain hammered against the corrugated iron roof of the abandoned warehouse, a relentless rhythm mirroring the relentless pursuit that had consumed Thomas for the past five years. He'd become a ghost, a whisper in the shadows, a phantom fueled by unwavering loyalty and a chilling efficiency honed by the military's brutal training regimen. His enhanced senses, a grotesque gift from Tempête, were both a blessing and a curse. He could hear a mouse squeak from across the street, smell the faintest trace of Irina's unique perfume a block away, and feel the tremor of Elara's approaching storm before a single cloud darkened the sky. This hyper-awareness was a constant, oppressive weight, amplifying the sounds of the city into a harshness of anxiety.

His first successes were swift and brutal. He tracked down Seraphina to a small village nestled in the Pyrenees Mountains, her telepathic abilities offering little defence against his superior speed and strength. The encounter was short and decisive. The military wanted her alive for interrogation, but the satisfaction of his success felt cold and hollow, leaving behind a lingering taste of ash and regret. He had been trained to eliminate threats, not to feel them.

Marcus proved a more elusive target. His pyrokinesis, initially erratic and uncontrolled, had become a terrifying weapon. Thomas chased him across the scorched landscapes of southern France, their clashes leaving trails of devastation in their wake. He cornered Marcus once in the ruins of a bombed-out church, but the young man's fury was a burning inferno, forcing Thomas into a strategic retreat. He learned to anticipate Marcus's volatile nature, to predict his fiery outbursts, turning the young mutant's unpredictable power against him. It was a brutal dance of destruction, a testament to the twisted game of cat and mouse that had become their lives.

Elara, however, remained the most formidable opponent. Her control over the weather was both unpredictable and devastating. She could summon blizzards that buried entire towns, unleash torrential downpours that turned city streets into raging rivers or conjure fierce winds that shredded everything in their path. Their encounters were epic battles against the forces of nature, waged amidst howling gales and blinding rain. Thomas learned to adapt, to utilize his enhanced strength and agility to navigate her violent attacks, but he often found himself battered and bruised, his body aching from the relentless onslaught of wind and water. He respected her power, almost feared it, a stark contrast to the cold efficiency he felt towards his other targets.

Irina, however, remained the true enigma. She was the mastermind, the architect of the escape, her intelligence far exceeding his own. She was a phantom, disappearing into the bustling crowds of Paris, leaving behind a trail of meticulously planned diversions and elaborate decoys. He had almost caught her several times, only to find himself chasing a carefully constructed illusion. Her escape routes were complex labyrinths, a testament to her strategic genius. He began to respect her, not as an opponent, but as a formidable strategist who constantly outwitted him. He could sense her nearness – the ghost of her intelligent mind brushing against his– but never quite close enough to grab.

His failures were as potent as his victories. The constant pressure, the weight of his mission, and the unrelenting pursuit gnawed at him. He was becoming a creature of habit, living in a perpetual state of high alert. He barely slept, surviving on meagre rations and adrenaline, haunted by the faces of his former colleagues, their powers a constant reminder of his own enhanced capabilities, a gift that had become a curse. Each successful capture brought a fleeting sense of satisfaction, quickly replaced by a deeper unease, a profound sense of loneliness, and a recognition that he was sacrificing his own humanity in the name of duty.

He began to question his orders to second-guess the military's intentions. The initial zeal, the blind faith in his mission, had started to erode. Doubts, like insidious whispers, began to invade his once-clear-cut world. Was he truly hunting monsters, or was he merely a weapon used and discarded at the whim of a callous military machine? The lines began to blur, the clarity of his purpose fading like old photographs exposed to too much light.

The five years had aged him beyond his years. The relentless pursuit, the constant tension, and the cold, damp nights spent tracking his prey had left their mark. His once-clear eyes, sharp and focused, were now shadowed by weariness and a deep-seated melancholy. The once-clean lines of his face were now etched with exhaustion and a hint of remorse. His body, though enhanced, bore the scars of countless battles, physical reminders of the price he paid for his loyalty. He was a soldier, but he was also a man, and even the most rigorously trained soldiers could not entirely suppress the human capacity for doubt and self-reflection.

Over those five years, Irina had skillfully woven a network of support for the escaped mutants. She had used her intelligence and resources to create a hidden infrastructure, a system of safe houses and secret communication channels that crisscrossed Europe, allowing her colleagues to move undetected to evade Thomas's relentless pursuit. Her understanding of human psychology and her ability to manipulate people and situations proved far more effective than any brute force could ever be. She was a spider at the centre of her web, weaving intricate strategies that constantly frustrated and confounded Thomas. He was the hunter, yet he felt like the hunted at times.

Elara, initially terrified and vulnerable, had learned to harness her powers with chilling proficiency. She was no longer merely reacting to her abilities; she was actively shaping them, using them to her advantage. She learned to control her storms, to focus their power, to unleash targeted bursts of wind and rain, turning the environment into a formidable weapon. Her adaptability and resilience transformed her from a mere escapee into a powerful force to be reckoned with.

Seraphina, her telepathic abilities initially weak and easily suppressed, had strengthened her powers through years of careful practice and relentless self-improvement. She could now reach out and touch the minds of multiple individuals simultaneously, picking up on their emotions, their anxieties, and their secrets. She used this power not only to anticipate Thomas's movements but also to build a powerful network of allies and loyal supporters who were willing to risk everything to protect the escaped mutants.

Marcus, haunted by the destructive power he possessed, struggled initially to control his pyrokinesis. He spent countless nights alone, wrestling with his fiery abilities, learning to channel his rage, to transform his fear and anger into something more focused, more controlled. He became a master of stealth, using shadows and darkness as his allies, his fiery power only unleashed as a last resort.

The five years were not merely years of relentless pursuit. They were also years of self-discovery, years of profound transformation for the escaped mutants, each learning to harness their powers, to adapt to their situation, to fight back against the relentless pressure of Thomas's pursuit. It became a war of slow destruction, a battle of wills and strategies, a chilling testament to the human capacity for both resilience and despair.

Irina's Network

The Parisian sewers, a labyrinthine underworld beneath the city of lights, became Irina's unlikely sanctuary. Years of relentless pursuit had forced her to develop an intricate network, a spiderweb of informants and safe houses woven through the underbelly of Paris. Her enhanced intellect, a terrifying weapon in the wrong hands, now served as a shield, allowing her to anticipate Thomas's movements to predict his strategies with chilling accuracy. She wasn't merely surviving; she was thriving, building a fortress of secrecy that protected not only herself but her fellow escapees.

Her network wasn't built on coercion or fear but on a carefully cultivated trust. She understood the nuances of human interaction, the subtle cues that betrayed a person's true intentions. Her exceptional memory, a repository of countless faces, names, and details, allowed her to identify potential allies, gauge their loyalty, and exploit their vulnerabilities with surgical precision. She recruited individuals from the margins of society – artists, writers, musicians, and even criminals – those who lived in the shadows, those who understood the value of discretion and the price of betrayal.

Each contact was a carefully placed piece in a complex puzzle. A bookbinder with access to hidden compartments in old volumes served as a secure communication hub. A street artist, with his cryptic graffiti, relayed warnings and coded messages. A network of seemingly innocuous cafes and bars – each with a specific signal, a particular song, or an inconspicuous gesture – became safe houses, temporary refuges where Irina and her colleagues could gather, plan their movements, and exchange information.

Elara, with her volatile power to control the weather, initially seemed an unlikely asset. Her unpredictable nature made her a liability, her outbursts sometimes drawing unwanted attention. But Irina saw her potential. She realized Elara's volatile power was also a weapon of concealment. A sudden downpour, a blinding fog, a fierce gust of wind – all could obscure movements, mask escape routes, and create diversions. Irina used her intellect to channel Elara's power, ensuring that the storms stayed focused on protecting their network. She had devised a system of coded signals through subtle variations in the weather patterns to communicate with Elara from afar. A change in wind direction, a sudden shift in cloud cover, and even the intensity of a rainstorm all carried hidden messages of urgency or safety.

Seraphina, with her telepathic abilities, was the network's unseen sentinel. She acted as an early warning system, detecting Thomas's approach from miles away, relaying his movements to Irina through subtle mental suggestions. Seraphina's connection to the network was discreet. Only Irina knew the full extent of her abilities, and Seraphina's contribution was never obvious to the other members. The other members only knew that their meetings were always seemingly unplanned and always safe.

The greatest challenge was maintaining secrecy and avoiding detection. The military's relentless pursuit left Irina constantly on edge. She had to anticipate Thomas's every move, to anticipate his attempts to unravel her carefully constructed web. She had a system of counter-surveillance in place, a network of "eyes and ears" who observed and reported on unusual activity. Each meeting location was selected meticulously. Each communication channel was tested rigorously.

Irina's intelligence wasn't just about gathering information; it was about interpreting it, anticipating patterns, and preempting her adversaries' actions. She developed intricate escape routes through the city's labyrinthine streets and hidden passages, using her knowledge of the city's architecture and its hidden history to create impossible escapes. She turned the city's crowded streets and alleyways into a playground of deception, using her intellect and the network's resources to move the other mutants undetected.

The network wasn't static. It was dynamic, constantly evolving, adapting to the ever-changing landscape of the pursuit. New members were recruited, old ones were replaced, and communication channels were constantly reviewed and adjusted. Irina saw each member as a crucial part of a larger organism, each playing a vital role in the survival of the group. She fostered a sense of loyalty and mutual respect among her network, creating a community of shared goals and strengthening their bonds in the face of ever-present danger.

The network, however, wasn't without its internal tensions. Marcus, with his volatile pyrokinetic abilities, was a constant source of concern. His impulsive nature and unpredictable outbursts threatened to expose the entire operation. Irina had to manage his volatile temperament to channel his destructive power into a defensive asset. She'd learned that Marcus responded well to a sense of purpose, and she subtly manipulated his perceptions, making him feel instrumental in the network's defence. His unpredictable power also served a strange but effective purpose; it created diversions, making Thomas question which of the members he was chasing.

Beyond the immediate threats posed by Thomas and the military, Irina had to contend with internal conflicts. The constant threat of discovery and the emotional toll of living in hiding created friction among the members of the network. Jealousy, mistrust, and simmering resentment threatened to undermine the fragile unity of the group. Irina's skill in manipulating and motivating the different personalities proved crucial in keeping everyone focused on their shared survival. She learned to play her contacts against each other, using their ambitions and insecurities to maintain her position of power and subtly influence them to her purposes.

Despite her genius, Irina found herself increasingly haunted by her past. Her escape from Tempete's clutches had not erased the trauma she had endured. The memories of the experiments, the brutality of her training, and the constant fear of capture lingered. This internal struggle sometimes made her ruthless, as she relentlessly prioritized survival for herself and her network. She often found herself making choices she knew were morally grey but necessary for the survival of her group. The line between survival and ruthlessness was blurred. This constant push and pull created a weight she bore constantly, always wondering if the price of their survival was worth the cost.

The years of pursuit were not just a physical and emotional battle for the escaped mutants. It was also a testament to Irina's exceptional intellect, her strategic brilliance, and her unwavering determination. Her network wasn't just a system of escape; it was a testament to her courage, resilience, and, ultimately, her leadership. It was a living, breathing entity, constantly evolving, adapting, and surviving. It was a reflection of Irina herself – a complex, paradoxical figure, brilliant and ruthless, resourceful and haunted. In the heart of Paris's shadowy underbelly, she had built a fortress of defiance against a relentless enemy, demonstrating the remarkable human ability to adapt, endure, and ultimately prevail. The city, with its intricate network of streets and sewers, provided her with the perfect camouflage and the tools to continue the fight, one step ahead of her pursuer, always one step ahead of the impending doom. The years were relentless, the battles were never-ending, but Irina's network held firm. This was her war, and she was winning, for now. The future, however, remained as uncertain as the Parisian weather.

Elara's Adaptation

The relentless Parisian rain mirrored Elara's internal storm. Five years. Five years of running, of hiding, of mastering the terrifying power that pulsed within her, a power that had once felt like a curse, now a shield, a weapon, a part of her very being. Unlike Irina, whose sanctuary was the intricate labyrinth of the Parisian sewers, Elara found refuge in the city's unpredictable weather. The skies above Paris became her canvas, her battlefield, her ally. She learned to manipulate the rain, not just to shield herself from pursuers, but to use it as a weapon, a blinding curtain, a roaring torrent that could sweep away any who dared to follow.

Her early attempts were clumsy, uncontrolled bursts of wind and rain, erratic displays of power that betrayed her position rather than concealing it. She remembers one harrowing incident in the Tuileries Garden, a desperate attempt to escape Thomas, resulting in a surge that flooded the pathways and sent terrified citizens scrambling for cover. The memory still stings; it was a reckless act born of fear and inexperience. But it was also a turning point. The near capture drove her to refine her control, to study the subtle shifts in atmospheric pressure, the delicate dance of wind currents. She devoured meteorological texts, poring over antiquated charts and scientific papers, her enhanced senses absorbing information at an astonishing rate. Libraries became her sanctuaries, not the hushed, scholarly sanctuaries of the wealthy, but the forgotten corners of the city's archives, repositories of neglected knowledge.

Her understanding of her abilities evolved from raw power to calculated precision. She learned to conjure localized storms, pinpoint blasts of wind that could knock an opponent off balance, or chilling gusts that could freeze pursuers in place. She could summon rain as a shield, a wall of water that deflected bullets and masked her movements. She learned to mimic the subtle changes in atmospheric pressure, masking her presence and making herself practically invisible.

The Seine, with its ever-shifting currents and unpredictable moods, became her classroom. She'd spend hours on its banks, manipulating the river's flow, creating miniature whirlpools and currents, practising her control. The water, responsive to her will, was both a mirror and a teacher, reflecting her progress and revealing the nuances of her power. She discovered that the river itself was a living entity, responding to her influence in ways she didn't fully understand. The subtle feedback, the way the water shifted and flowed in response to her manipulation, allowed her to refine her technique to develop an almost symbiotic relationship with the elements.

Her knowledge, however, wasn't limited to the scientific. She learned from the city itself, from the street urchins who lived on its margins, and from the old women who sold herbs and potions in the shadowy marketplaces. She learned to read the signs, the subtle shifts in the energy of the city, the unspoken currents of fear and anxiety that followed her trail. She learned to become one with the city's rhythms, to blend into the urban landscape, to disappear into the crowd, to be both a part of it and separate from it. She was the storm, unpredictable, powerful, yet strangely beautiful in its destructive glory.

The years of pursuit forced her to become a strategist, a schemer, and a master of deception. She understood Thomas was relentless, a relentless force of nature in his own right, trained to hunt and to kill. His enhanced senses made him a nightmare to evade. So, Elara learned to manipulate not only the weather but also the perceptions of her pursuers. She created illusions, using fog and rain to obscure her movements, misdirecting Thomas, leading him on wild goose chases through the labyrinthine streets of Paris. She'd leave false trails, manipulating the wind to carry her scent in the wrong direction. She'd use her powers to trigger seemingly random events, drawing attention away from her true location.

One particularly daring escape involved a carefully orchestrated storm during a crowded marketplace. Using the chaos as cover, she manipulated the rain to create a localized flash flood, using the surging water as a barrier between herself and

Thomas while simultaneously using the storm's fury to create a diversion, giving her ample opportunity to vanish into the swirling mass of people, the wind and rain obscuring her escape route.

But her adaptation went beyond the physical. The constant fear the relentless pursuit shaped her personality. The carefree spirit she'd possessed before the escape had vanished, replaced by a guarded vigilance, a sharp awareness that was always on edge. She was constantly scanning her environment, anticipating threats, and reading the nuances of human behavior. Trust became a luxury she couldn't afford. Every encounter, every interaction, was fraught with caution. She carried the weight of years of fear and trauma on her shoulders.

Yet, amidst the fear and the constant threat, a resilience bloomed. Elara didn't break; she adapted, she evolved, she became stronger. Her connection with nature, with the power of the storms, became a source of strength, a link to something larger than herself. It was in the unpredictable power of the elements that she found a reflection of her own spirit – unpredictable, chaotic, yet ultimately powerful.

The Parisian skies were her constant companion, a witness to her struggle, a symbol of her resilience, and a reflection of her ever-growing mastery over her abilities. And though the pursuit never ceased, Elara had not only survived but thrived. She had become the storm, a force of nature that even Thomas would find difficult to control. The years of pursuit had shaped her into something formidable, a testament to human resilience and the power of adaptation, leaving even the ever-vigilant Thomas guessing at where she would strike next. The city of Paris, with its intricate maze of streets, was her battleground, and the ever-changing weather her weapon. And in this crucible of fear and relentless pursuit, Elara, the weather weaver, had found her true strength, a strength that rivaled even the fury of the storms themselves. She was not merely surviving; she was becoming something more, something formidable, something unstoppable. The shadows of the city held her secrets, and the unpredictable weather veiled her movements. But in the heart of the storm, Elara's spirit burned bright, unyielding, a beacon of defiance against the forces that sought to destroy her. The future remained uncertain, a tortuous sea mirroring the turbulent emotions within her, but Elara, mistress of the storm, was ready. She would face whatever came next with the fury of a storm and the unwavering resilience of a survivor. Her transformation was complete. She was no longer just a mutant; she was a force of nature.

Seraphina's Growing Power

The garret room, cramped and smelling faintly of mildew and old paper, was Seraphina's sanctuary. It wasn't luxurious, far from it. The single window, forever smeared with grime, offered a paltry view of the Parisian rooftops, a vista punctuated by the occasional chimney pot and the distant, mournful cry of a pigeon. Yet, within these humble confines, Seraphina cultivated a power that dwarfed the grandeur of any palace.

Five years. Five years since the escape, five years of honing the terrifying, exhilarating gift – or curse, depending on the day – of telepathy. Initially, it had been a torrent of noise, a chaotic symphony of thoughts, emotions, and fears crashing against her consciousness. The cacophony of the city, the anxieties of its inhabitants, and the whispers and shouts had nearly overwhelmed her. She had retreated into herself, burying herself in the quietude of the garret, seeking refuge from the relentless onslaught of mental impressions.

But solitude, while necessary, was not sufficient. Seraphina needed to learn control, to filter the noise, to focus her attention. She began with small exercises, focusing on the thoughts of a single individual, a passerby on the street below, a vendor hawking his wares, and a couple arguing in hushed tones. Gradually, she learned to discern individual voices from the collective murmur to isolate specific thoughts from the overwhelming tidal wave of mental energy. The process was excruciating, a mental equivalent of learning to walk on a tightrope. One misstep, one moment of distraction, and she would be swept away by the torrent of other minds.

Her training was unorthodox, her teachers the teeming millions of Paris. The city became her laboratory, its inhabitants her unwilling subjects. She practiced her craft in the bustling markets, the crowded cafes, and the dimly lit alleyways. She learned to distinguish between surface thoughts and deeper emotions, to perceive intentions and desires hidden beneath layers of pretense. She could feel the simmering resentment of a shop owner cheated by a customer, the unspoken longing of a young couple stealing a secret kiss, and the desperate fear of a homeless man huddled in a doorway. It was an education in the human condition, a brutal, intimate exploration of the soul laid bare.

The refinement of her telepathic skills wasn't merely about eavesdropping; it was about influence. Subtle at first, her influence grew with practice. A whispered suggestion here, a subtly shifted perception there. She could nudge a conversation in a desired direction, plant a seed of doubt in a pursuer's mind, and redirect the attention of a potential threat. This mastery was a dangerous tool, one she wielded with caution, aware of the ethical implications of her power. She walked a tightrope, balancing the need for self-preservation with the moral compass that, despite the horrors she had endured, remained stubbornly intact.

Her newfound abilities didn't come without a cost. The constant bombardment of thoughts and emotions, even with her improved control, took a toll. Nights were spent battling exhaustion, the mental equivalent of physical fatigue. Headaches, relentless and debilitating, became her constant companion. Sometimes, the sheer volume of mental noise threatened to overwhelm her, sending her into a state of catatonic withdrawal, a chilling reminder of the fragility of her mental defenses.

Yet, the fear was a powerful motivator. The memory of Thomas's relentless pursuit, the chilling efficiency with which he hunted down his former colleagues, fueled her determination. She knew that he possessed an uncanny ability to track them, an almost supernatural awareness that bordered on the telepathic. She believed, with a chilling certainty, that he could sense their fear, their anxieties, their vulnerabilities. That understanding shaped her strategy, driving her to perfect her control, to become a ghost in the minds of those around her, and to disappear not just physically but mentally as well.

Seraphina's influence wasn't limited to individuals. She learned to tap into the collective consciousness of the city itself, a vast and chaotic network of interconnected minds. It was like listening to a gigantic, ever-shifting cluster of thoughts, a swirling vortex of emotions. She could sense the mood of a neighbourhood, the undercurrents of anxiety or excitement that rippled through the city. This awareness was a powerful asset, allowing her to anticipate events, to avoid detection, to maneuver through the city's crowded streets like a phantom.

Her growing power, however, brought with it a growing sense of responsibility. The ability to influence the thoughts and emotions of others was a double-edged sword. She had seen firsthand the devastating consequences of unchecked power, the brutal experiments of Tempête, the merciless pursuit orchestrated by the military. She vowed never to abuse her abilities, to never succumb to the temptation to control or manipulate others for her own gain. But maintaining that vow in the face of such overwhelming power was a constant struggle.

The temptation to use her abilities for revenge, to turn the tables on Thomas, was always present, a dark whisper in the back of her mind. But the memories of her own torment, the pain inflicted upon her and her colleagues, tempered that desire. She knew that succumbing to vengeance would only continue the cycle of violence, only lead to further suffering. She would survive, she would evade Thomas, but she would do so without compromising her own moral integrity.

As the years passed, Seraphina transformed from a victim into a survivor, from a hunted fugitive into a master of her own destiny. The garret, once a refuge from the noise of the city, became a crucible in which she forged her power, honing her skills with unwavering determination and a fierce sense of self-preservation. Paris, once a terrifying labyrinth of threats, became her training ground, a vast and ever-changing landscape in which she learned to navigate the treacherous currents of human consciousness. The city, with its millions of minds, became her teacher, her ally, and, ultimately, her weapon. Seraphina was no longer merely escaping; she was evolving, becoming something far more powerful, far more dangerous than she had ever imagined. And in the shadows of the city, the unseen mistress of minds prepared for what was to come. The game, she knew, was far from over. The hunt, a relentless dance of cat and mouse, continued. But Seraphina was no longer just running; she was planning her next move, one subtle thought at a time.

Marcus's Self-Discovery

The flickering candlelight danced across the primitive wooden walls of his cell, casting long, distorted shadows that mimicked the flames that pulsed beneath his skin. Five years. Five years he'd spent in this cold, damp purgatory, a prisoner of his own power, a victim of the cruel experiments that had twisted him into something inhuman. Five years since he'd last felt the warmth of the sun on his face, the comforting touch of another human being. Five years of fear, of self-loathing, of the constant, agonizing burn of his pyrokinesis.

Marcus had been a child when they'd taken him, a scared, confused boy who'd only recently discovered the terrifying potential simmering within him. The scientists – cold, emotionless figures in white coats – had reveled in his fear, exploiting it, pushing him to the brink of madness. They'd forced him to control his power, to weaponize it, turning him into a tool for their unspeakable ambitions. He remembered the searing pain, the agonizing burns, the feeling of his very soul being consumed by the fire within. He remembered the screams. His own screams and the screams of others.

Escape had been a desperate, chaotic scramble fueled by adrenaline and a primal need for survival. He'd burned his way out of that hellish laboratory, leaving behind a trail of devastation and the echoes of his tortured cries. But freedom had offered little solace. The world outside, once vibrant and full of wonder, now seemed like a hostile landscape, a place where he was an outcast, a monster.

He had learned to control the flames somewhat. To channel the raw, untamed energy that raged within him into something manageable, something... controlled. But the control was tenuous, always threatening to unravel, sending him into fits of uncontrollable rage with devastating consequences. He'd learned to survive by hiding, by living in the shadows, a ghost in his own city. He lived off scraps, his fear a constant companion. Even the briefest flicker of his power could bring down the wrath of the authorities upon him. The memory of the screams still echoed.

He'd spent his days scavenging, his nights hiding, the constant awareness of his power a heavy weight on his soul. He longed for connection, for companionship, but he knew that such things were impossible. He was a danger to himself and to everyone around him. His very existence was a curse. His only friend, if you could call it that, was the fire within him, a constant reminder of his monstrous nature. He spoke to it, sometimes, pleading with it, cursing it, begging for release.

Then, one bitterly cold night, huddled in a deserted alleyway, he saw her. A young woman, no older than himself, clutching a thin shawl against the biting wind, her eyes filled with an overwhelming sadness. She was shivering, her teeth chattering, her face pale and drawn. Marcus hesitated. He should have run. He should have kept hidden in the shadows, safe from the world and the world from him. But something in her eyes, something in her vulnerability, touched him.

He approached cautiously, the fire within him threatening to erupt. He didn't know what to expect, what to say. He offered her some of the meager scraps he'd managed to scrounge. The woman, her eyes wide with surprise, accepted his offering with a shaky hand. As she ate, her eyes remained on him. A fear, but also something else, a flicker of understanding.

That night, for the first time in years, Marcus felt a flicker of hope. He felt a connection to another human being, a connection that transcended his fear and his self-loathing. He discovered he could control his pyrokinesis better in the presence of this woman as if her presence itself was a grounding force that calmed the raging inferno within him. She didn't recoil from his presence. She didn't scream. She simply accepted him, flaws and all.

Her name was Anya. She lived on the fringes of society, eking out a meager existence as a street artist, her paintings bursting with vibrant colors and raw emotion. She saw something in Marcus —

not a monster, not a weapon, but a broken man struggling to find his way. She didn't judge him, didn't fear him. She helped him to heal.

Anya introduced him to others who lived outside the rigid societal structures, others who'd been cast aside, broken, and rejected by society. Among them, he found a sense of community. They saw not his power but him. For the first time, he saw himself not as a monster but as someone who possessed a power he could learn to harness, to control, to use for good. He learned to use his abilities to heal, to help others, to protect the vulnerable. He learned to fight, to defend himself and his community from those who would harm them.

Through her gentle kindness and her unwavering belief in him, Anya helped Marcus unlock a new aspect of himself. She helped him confront the trauma of his past to understand the depth of his suffering. This was a long and difficult journey, fraught with emotional turmoil. The memories of the experiments, of the pain, of the fear resurfaced, overwhelming him at times. But Anya's unwavering support provided him with the courage to confront those demons.

He spent hours with Anya, pouring out his heart. He told her about his stolen childhood, the horrors he had endured in the laboratory, and the relentless pursuit by Thomas. Anya listened patiently, without judgment. She recognized the pain in his eyes, the weight of his guilt, and she helped him understand that what he had endured was not his fault. It was a brutal process, reliving his traumas, reliving his fear and uncertainty. But in the telling of his stories, he found release. He could let go of the pain and guilt and begin to acknowledge that he could be more than the weapon he was made into.

His powers, he found, were connected to his emotions. Intense fear or anger would ignite uncontrollable flames. But joy, love, and compassion produced a warm, gentle glow. He discovered he could harness these positive emotions, using them to soothe the fire within to refine his control. He began to experiment, using his abilities to create warmth and light in the cold, dark corners of their makeshift community. He used his fire to help prepare meals, to keep them warm during the bitter winters, creating a sense of normalcy in their unusual community.

Anya taught him to channel his energies into creative expression. She encouraged him to draw, to sculpt, to paint. He discovered a hidden talent for pottery, creating beautiful, unique pieces that were as unique as his own journey of self-discovery. He found solace in the tactile experience of moulding clay, of feeling the warmth of the earth between his fingers. The flames within him found a parallel in the fire of the kiln that helped shape his artwork. The process was therapeutic, a way to channel his potent power into a creative outlet, calming and focusing the destructive energy.

The years that followed were a testament to his transformation. He was no longer a hunted fugitive, consumed by fear and self-loathing. He was Marcus, a survivor, a creator, a man who had found his place in the world. He found his identity not in his power but in his heart. He'd found peace, a kind of fragile equilibrium, a balance between the fire within and the compassion within his soul. He still carried the scars of the past, both visible and invisible, but he carried them with dignity. He had become something more than a weapon. He became a protector, a symbol of hope in a world riddled with darkness. His journey wasn't over, but it had changed. His life was still precarious. Still lived on the fringes of society. But within that precarious existence, he found something truly profound: a purpose. He was no longer a prisoner of his own power. He was its master. And in mastering it, he had mastered himself.

Chapter 6: A Gathering Storm

Thomas's Growing Doubts

The Parisian rain hammered against the corrugated iron roof of the dilapidated warehouse, a relentless rhythm mirroring the turmoil brewing within Thomas. Five years. Five years he'd spent as the military's instrument of vengeance, a phantom hunting the ghosts of Tempête. Five years of relentless pursuit of tracking his former colleagues across the treacherous landscape of a war-torn Europe, a landscape both familiar and alien in its devastation. He'd excelled, his enhanced senses a cruel gift, allowing him to anticipate their moves, to smell their fear, to taste the desperation clinging to their skin. Yet, with each successful hunt, the victory felt hollower, the satisfaction replaced by an unsettling emptiness.

It had started subtly, a tremor in his usually unwavering obedience, a flicker of doubt in his mission. It wasn't the brutality of his training that haunted him – that was ingrained, a brutal choreography he performed without question. It was the faces of his quarry. He remembered snatches of conversations from the Tempête laboratory, the shared anxieties, and the fleeting moments of friendship before the military's iron fist crushed their spirit. He saw Elara's wide, frightened eyes as he'd cornered her in the ruins of a bombed-out church in Prague, the raw terror reflecting the storm brewing within her. He recalled the fleeting glimpse of Seraphina's anguish as she desperately tried to shield herself and her companions from his pursuit. Even Marcus, a volatile force of nature, had looked at him with a mixture of fear and…understanding. A haunting understanding.

His enhanced senses were a double-edged sword. He could hear the faintest whisper of their escape routes, smell the lingering scent of their presence, and even taste the residual fear they had left behind. But these senses also amplified the echoes of their past, the shared experiences that linked them – a brotherhood forged in the crucible of Tempête, shattered by the military's ruthlessness. He'd been trained to ignore empathy, to suppress any

97

feelings beyond loyalty to his superiors, yet the memories, once muted and distant, were now gaining clarity and power, invading his consciousness and shattering the illusion of his unquestioning devotion.

The military's methods were brutal, honed to turn the mutants into weapons – but there was an underlying failure in their calculations. They'd focused on physical and tactical training, ignoring the inherent human aspect of their creations. They underestimated the bond that had formed between these individuals. In his relentless pursuit, Thomas had witnessed glimpses of this bond - a silent communication between Elara and Seraphina, a subtle protective strategy among the group, a kind of unspoken language he'd initially dismissed as coincidence. His training could suppress his emotions, but it couldn't erase his memories.

One evening, in a small village tucked away in the Swiss Alps, as he tracked Elara, he stumbled upon a hidden network of resistance fighters. These weren't the sophisticated strategists of Irina's circle but ordinary people, driven by a common cause: the protection of those deemed "different" from the rigid norms established by the war. They provided Elara with shelter, sustenance, information, and a fragile sense of security. It was here, witnessing their shared humanity, that the first significant crack appeared in Thomas's unbreakable façade.

He had overheard their discussions - whispers about a planned rebellion, a counter-offensive spearheaded by Irina, a daring attempt to strike at the heart of the military's operation. Their conviction, their unwavering faith in Elara and the others, seemed to mock his own unquestioning loyalty to the military, its rigid structure now seeming to him both suffocating and absurd in the face of such genuine resilience.

The military had told him that these mutants were dangerous, unpredictable threats to the very fabric of society. But in the hushed conversations of the villagers, he heard a different narrative – a narrative of survival, of resilience in the face of persecution, of individuals fighting for their right to exist. The villagers' unwavering support for the Tempête mutants created an unsettling dissonance, a stark contrast to his own cold pursuit. Was he really hunting dangerous enemies or simply eliminating those who had been rendered outcasts in a society unable to accept their otherness?

The memory of his own training haunted him. The endless drills, the brutal conditioning, the systematic suppression of his own emotions. The military hadn't just honed his skills; they had methodically dehumanized him, transforming him into a living weapon devoid of his own moral compass. He was a hunter, a killer, but the prey he stalked were far more human than his handlers ever were.

He began to question the very nature of his mission. He questioned the legitimacy of the military's claim that these individuals were a threat. He'd seen their fear, their vulnerability, their desperate attempts to survive. He had seen the ingenuity of Irina, the raw power of Marcus, the quiet strength of Elara, and the acute empathy of Seraphina. They were all victims of a system that created them and then sought to control and destroy them. He was no different. He was also a victim.

The rain continued its relentless assault, mirroring the growing storm within him. He was no longer merely a hunter; he was becoming something else entirely – a man wrestling with his conscience, a soldier questioning his orders, a weapon contemplating its own destruction. The weight of his actions, the burden of his past, pressed down on him with crushing force. The rigid lines of his loyalty were beginning to fracture. He was losing his footing, caught in a moral quagmire of his own making. He knew, with a chilling certainty, that the next encounter wouldn't just be a hunt. It would be a reckoning. A reckoning not just with his former colleagues but with himself. The gathering storm wasn't just outside; it raged within him, threatening to overwhelm his carefully constructed identity and unleash something unpredictable, something he hadn't even begun to comprehend. The question was, could he survive the storm, or would it consume him entirely?

Irinas Counteroffensive

The flickering gaslight cast long shadows across Irina's cramped attic room in Prague. Rain lashed against the windowpanes, a relentless percussion accompanying the frantic scribbling of her pen. Scattered across the worn wooden table were maps, blueprints, and coded messages – the meticulous planning of a war waged not with armies but with intellect. Five years. Five years since she'd escaped the clutches of the military, five years of living in the shadows, of constantly looking over her shoulder. Five years since she'd last seen Thomas, the relentless hunter, a specter of her past, fueled by obedience and enhanced senses. But Irina wasn't defined by fear. Fear was a luxury she couldn't afford. She was a strategist, and her weapon wasn't brute force but a sharp mind capable of outmaneuvering even the most formidable foe.

Her escape hadn't been a flight driven by panic but a calculated retreat, a strategic withdrawal. She'd used her exceptional intelligence to anticipate the military's next moves, to predict their hunting patterns, and to vanish before they could close in. She'd cultivated a network of informants, a hidden web of allies across Europe, people who understood the nature of the threat they all faced and the dangers of the technology that birthed them. They were the remnants of Tempête, each survivor carrying the burden of their past and the hope for a future free from military control.

The meticulous organization of her counter-offensive began subtly. First, she'd established secure communication channels, using a complex system of coded messages delivered via trusted couriers, avoiding the numerous military surveillances. This involved recruiting and training individuals skilled in cryptography and covert operations, building a resilient network that could withstand infiltration. She'd spent countless hours studying military strategy, exploiting their weaknesses while building on her strengths, her unique ability to process and analyze information at an unparalleled speed.

Her initial targets weren't military strongholds or heavily guarded facilities. Her campaign started with a series of smaller, more surgical strikes designed to sow discord and confusion within the military ranks. Leaks of sensitive information, carefully planted disinformation, sabotage of key logistical operations - each act of calculated disruption served to erode the military's confidence and expose their vulnerabilities. These operations required pinpoint accuracy and impeccable timing, and only individuals with specialized skills could execute them effectively. This phase of the counter-offensive, designed to undermine the military from within, wasn't about inflicting direct physical harm but about creating a climate of uncertainty and paranoia, making it difficult for them to concentrate their forces.

The next stage involved exploiting the very technology that created them. Irina remembered the countless experiments, the painful procedures, and the unwavering ambition of Dr. Reed, the man who had refused to abandon the Tempête project. She knew the limitations of their enhancements; she knew the vulnerabilities of the military's training regimes. And she used this knowledge to her advantage. Her intelligence was not only a tool for strategic planning but also a weapon for exploiting technological and operational weaknesses. She identified gaps in the military's security protocols, vulnerabilities in their communication networks, and potential points of failure in their weapon systems.

Months turned into a year. The tide began to subtly shift. Rumors of internal conflicts within the military spread like wildfire. Supplies dwindled, communications faltered, and morale plummeted. Irina, a silent architect of this chaos, watched from the shadows, meticulously orchestrating each move. Her network, carefully cultivated and fiercely loyal, was her most valuable asset. They were scientists, engineers, hackers, and ex-military personnel, all united by a shared sense of betrayal and a burning desire for retribution.

The final stage of her plan was bold, audacious, and incredibly risky. It required a direct confrontation with the military, a gamble that could cost her everything. She needed to strike at the heart of the military's operation, at the very source of their power, their scientific prowess, and their technological advancements. This was the culmination of years of planning, a meticulously crafted strategy built on intelligence, deception, and the sheer force of her intellect.

Irina's strategy involved a multi-pronged attack. One team, led by a former military engineer who possessed intimate knowledge of the military's internal security systems, would infiltrate their main research facility. Their objective was not destruction but the acquisition of critical information: research data, schematics, and anything that could expose the military's weaknesses and provide them with an edge. Another team, comprised of experts in computer science and cryptography, would simultaneously launch a cyberattack, targeting the military's communication networks and disrupting their operations.

The most critical element of Irina's plan revolved around manipulating the military's own enhanced soldiers, turning their weapons against them. Through a carefully designed disinformation campaign, she planted false information designed to sow dissent and mistrust among the ranks of the enhanced individuals, exploiting existing conflicts and divisions. This was a high-stakes gamble, playing on the psychological vulnerabilities of individuals accustomed to unquestioning obedience.

The night of the counter-offensive was filled with a tense energy. Rain continued to lash the city, mirroring the storm brewing within Irina's heart. Her own enhanced intelligence was strained, processing a torrent of data, coordinating her teams, and anticipating the military's response. But she was ready. Five years of meticulous planning, strategic maneuvering, of calculated risks had led to this moment. This wasn't simply an act of rebellion; it was a reclamation of power, a fight for survival, a fight for a future free from the autocracy of unchecked scientific ambition.

The infiltration of the research facility went smoothly. The engineer's intimate knowledge of the facility's security protocols proved invaluable. They bypassed security systems with ease, accessing restricted areas and retrieving crucial data. Simultaneously, the cyberattack crippled the military's communication networks, plunging them into chaos. Reports of internal conflicts among the enhanced soldiers began flooding Irina's communication channels, confirming that the disinformation campaign was working.

The military's response was swift and brutal. They scrambled to contain the chaos, but their efforts were hampered by the disorganization and internal strife. The combined effect of the infiltration, the cyberattack, and the psychological warfare left them reeling, their normally well-oiled machine grinding to a halt. But it wasn't simply a battle of technology and strategy; it was a battle of wills, a clash between the unchecked ambition of the military and the desperate fight for the survival of the Tempête mutants.

The counter-offensive wasn't a clean victory nor a decisive defeat. It was a bloody, chaotic clash, a turning point in the ongoing war between the enhanced individuals and the military. It was a war that wouldn't be won overnight, but one fought with intelligence, courage, and a burning desire to reclaim their freedom. The rain eventually stopped, and the city emerged from the darkness, a new dawn breaking, even though the war was far from over. Irina, still in Prague, looked towards the horizon, ready to continue her fight, knowing that her journey, and that of her fellow Tempête survivors, was far from over. The fight for their freedom, for their right to exist, was only beginning. And Irina, the brilliant strategist, would lead them into the unknown.

Elara's Desperate Gamble

The biting Parisian wind whipped Elara's hair across her face as she stood perched atop the Notre Dame Cathedral, the gargoyles seeming to leer down at her from their stony perches. Below, the city sprawled, a labyrinth of cobblestone streets and shadowed alleys, a stage set for her desperate gamble. Five years. Five years since the escape, five years of hiding, of constantly feeling Thomas's presence like a chilling breath on her neck. He was relentless, a predator honed by the military's brutal training, his enhanced senses a constant threat. Irina's meticulously planned counter-offensive had bought them time, a fleeting reprieve in a war that showed no sign of ending. But it wasn't enough. Thomas was closing in.

Her fingers, calloused from years of concealed work and harsh living, tightened around the small, intricately carved wooden box she held. Inside lay not weapons but tools – carefully calibrated instruments designed to amplify and focus her weather manipulation abilities. She hadn't created them in the sterile labs of Tempête but in the cramped, makeshift workshops of the Parisian underworld, relying on scavenged parts and ingenuity honed by necessity. These weren't the sophisticated devices the military had provided; these were born of desperation, fueled by a fierce will to survive.

Tonight, she wasn't just fighting for her life. She was fighting for the lives of her remaining comrades. She knew that Thomas was hunting them systematically, working his way down the list, each kill a chilling confirmation of his unwavering obedience. She had to stop him, to disrupt his relentless pursuit before it was too late. And she knew the only way to do it was to strike at the heart of his operation – to strike at him directly.

Elara closed her eyes, focusing on the swirling currents of air that surrounded her, feeling the subtle shifts in atmospheric pressure and the whispers of the wind. She could feel the city breathing, its pulse echoing in the rhythm of the wind. She was one with the storm, a conductor of its raw power. This wasn't a gift; it was a burden, a constant awareness of the unpredictable forces of nature. But tonight, she would harness that power, wielding it as a weapon of defiance.

Her plan was audacious, bordering on suicidal. She aimed to create a localized, highly intense weather phenomenon – a miniature storm – focused directly on the location where Thomas was believed to be operating. It was a calculated risk. She could miss her target entirely, or worse, her powers could overwhelm her, leaving her incapacitated or worse. But inaction was equal to suicide, slow death by a thousand cuts, inflicted by the ever-present fear of Thomas's inevitable arrival.

Taking a deep breath, Elara opened the box, revealing a series of meticulously crafted crystals and metallic resonators. Each piece hummed faintly with energy, amplifying her own bio-electrical field. With practiced movements, she assembled the devices, her fingers moving with the precision of a surgeon. This wasn't magic; it was science, albeit science pushed to its absolute limits, a risky dance on the edge of chaos. She felt the familiar tingling sensation in her fingertips, the surge of power building within her, a potent force that both exhilarated and terrified her.

The city lights twinkled below, oblivious to the brewing storm above. Elara focused her attention, drawing strength from the very air she breathed. She visualized the target location – a deserted warehouse on the outskirts of the city, a place known for its underground activities, a place she suspected Thomas was using as a temporary base. She had to be precise. A single miscalculation could mean devastation for innocent civilians.

She began to channel her power, the crystals glowing with an ethereal light as they resonated with her bio-energy. The wind intensified, howling around her like a pack of hungry wolves. Dark clouds gathered overhead, blotting out the stars, their ominous presence a mirror of the turmoil raging within her. The air grew heavy and thick with the scent of ozone and anticipation.

The first sign of her power manifesting was a subtle shift in the wind patterns, a ripple in the otherwise calm night. Then, with a sudden, violent gust, the wind intensified into a howling gale, rain lashing down, transforming the city into a watery chaos. Elara gritted her teeth, pushing herself harder, the strain evident in the sweat beading on her forehead. Her vision blurred slightly as she struggled to maintain control. This was beyond anything she had ever attempted before.

The storm she was summoning wasn't a simple storm. It was a meticulously crafted weapon, a focused vortex of wind and rain, designed to incapacitate, not destroy. She didn't want to kill Thomas; she wanted to subdue him, to buy time for her fellow Tempête survivors to escape and regroup. The thought provided a necessary focus, helping her maintain her control amidst the escalating chaos.

The wind roared, a deafening cacophony that seemed to shake the very foundations of the ancient cathedral. Rain lashed down with such rage that the city lights below were all but extinguished, swallowed by the torrential downpour. Lightning cracked across the sky, illuminating the swirling vortex she had created, a miniature replica of a hurricane, its center aimed directly at the warehouse.

As the storm reached its peak, Elara felt a wave of exhaustion wash over her, her body trembling with the effort. She had pushed her powers to their absolute limit. She had risked everything – her own life, the safety of the city – for a chance to turn the tide of this relentless war.

The storm raged for what felt like an eternity, a frenzy of destructive power. Then, as suddenly as it began, it subsided, leaving behind a trail of destruction, the city drenched and battered, the air still heavy with the lingering scent of ozone. Elara collapsed, her body spent, gasping for breath. She had done it. She had bought them time. But the cost had been steep.

As the first rays of dawn pierced through the remaining clouds, painting the sky in hues of pink and orange, Elara looked out at the ravaged city below, a grim reminder of the power she wielded, a power that could create and destroy with equal ease. The war wasn't over, not by a long shot. But for now, they had survived. And in the aftermath of her desperate gamble, a fragile hope flickered in the darkness, a hope for a future where they could reclaim their lives and their freedom from the shadow of Thomas's relentless pursuit. The fight for survival continued, but for now, the storm had passed.

Seraphina's Vision

The flickering gaslight cast long shadows across Seraphina's cramped attic room, the Parisian night pressing in on her like a suffocating blanket. She sat hunched over a worn, leather-bound book, its pages filled with arcane symbols and faded ink – a desperate attempt to understand the chaotic surges of psychic energy that plagued her. The escape from the military compound had left her raw and vulnerable, the psychic echoes of their brutal training still resonating within her mind. The constant, low hum of Thomas's presence, the ever-present threat of his enhanced senses, was a heavy weight on her soul.

Tonight, however, the hum was different. Louder, sharper, laced with a terrifying clarity. It wasn't just the usual, unsettling proximity; it was a wave, a tsunami of psychic energy emanating not from Thomas himself but from a distant yet intensely felt location. She closed her eyes, focusing, shielding her mind from the relentless noise of the city, trying to pinpoint the source, to filter through the psychic static.

The image came to her suddenly, a blinding flash of light followed by a chillingly clear vision. It was a desolate landscape, a stark contrast to the familiar cobblestone streets of Paris. A vast, barren plain stretched before her. The ground cracked and scorched as if by a relentless fire. In the distance, a colossal structure rose, a grotesque parody of human architecture, its jagged edges scraping against the bruised sky. It pulsed with a malevolent energy; a throbbing heart of darkness that echoed the fear she felt deep within her own being.

This wasn't just a premonition; it was a tangible vision, a glimpse into a future she desperately hoped to avert. Around the structure, figures clashed, figures she recognized instinctively: Elara, her control over the elements strained to its absolute limit; Irina, her sharp mind frantically attempting to strategize against an impossible foe; and Marcus, his pyrokinetic abilities unleashed in a chaotic, desperate attempt to destroy the ominous building. But they were losing. Overwhelmed. Outmatched.

The vision shifted. She saw Thomas not as the relentless hunter she knew but as a pawn, a tool. His enhanced senses were dulled, his actions controlled by unseen forces emanating from within the dark structure. He was fighting not for himself but for whatever sinister power resided within that monstrous building. He moved with frightening efficiency, his movements precise and deadly, his eyes devoid of the humanity she remembered.

A wave of nausea washed over her. The image then focused on the building itself; its true nature, terrifying in its scope and implications, became apparent. It wasn't merely a structure; it was a machine, a colossal engine of destruction powered by a source of energy both unimaginable and terrifying. She felt a cold dread grip her heart as she witnessed the machine's activation. A blinding wave of energy erupted from its core, reaching out across the desolate landscape, promising devastation and obliteration.

The vision ended as abruptly as it began, leaving Seraphina gasping for breath, her body trembling with the residual psychic energy. The attic room swam back into focus, the gaslight flickering like a dying candle. Sweat beaded on her forehead, and her heart hammered against her ribs like a trapped bird. The weight of the vision pressed upon her, a crushing burden of foreboding.

She knew, with a certainty that chilled her to the bone, that this was no mere dream or hallucination. This was a warning. A glimpse into a future that was rapidly approaching, a future that threatened not only her and her fellow escapees but the very fabric of existence. She had to warn them. She had to find a way to prevent this catastrophic future from becoming a reality.

But how? The location in her vision was unknown, a desolate wasteland far removed from the familiar streets of Paris. The enemy, whoever or whatever resided within that ominous structure, was clearly powerful beyond imagination, capable of controlling even Thomas, a man whose enhanced senses and deadly skills made him an almost invincible adversary. The odds seemed impossible.

Seraphina reached for the worn leather book, its pages filled with half-understood symbols and cryptic notes, desperate for a clue, a hint, anything that might guide her. The book was more than a collection of arcane knowledge; it was a testament to Tempete's reckless ambition, a grim chronicle of their ill-fated quest to cure consumption and the terrible consequences that followed. It held the key to understanding the depth of their mistakes, a history she needed to unravel to prevent another far greater catastrophe.

She spent the rest of the night poring over the pages, searching for a pattern, a connection, anything that might link her vision to Tempete's experiments. She reread the fragmented notes detailing the creation of the memory-erasing serum, a project that seemed almost insignificant compared to the monstrous threat she had witnessed in her vision. Could the serum hold a clue? Could it be linked to the power source that fueled the apocalyptic machine?

As dawn approached, a chilling realization dawned on her. The desolate landscape in her vision bore a striking resemblance to the descriptions of the Siberian testing grounds, the remote location where Tempête had conducted their most dangerous experiments. Could the machine she had seen be a culmination of their work, a consequence of their unchecked ambition?

The thought sent a shiver down her spine. If the machine was indeed a product of Tempete's research, then it was likely guarded by remnants of the military, the same forces that had hunted them for years. Reaching the Siberian testing grounds would be a suicide mission, a journey fraught with peril and the ever-present threat of Thomas. Yet, failure was not an option. The fate of the world might depend on her willingness to face the storm.

Her mind raced, trying to formulate a plan. She knew she couldn't face this threat alone. She needed Irina's tactical brilliance, Elara's control over the elements, and Marcus's destructive pyrokinesis. But reaching them would be challenging. They were scattered, each living in hiding, their trust in each other frayed by years of relentless pursuit. Would they believe her vision? Would they risk everything to prevent a future so bleak, so terrifying?

The weight of responsibility was immense. The fate of the world rested on her shoulders, a burden she never asked for, a burden she wasn't sure she could bear. But as she looked out at the rising sun, casting its pale light across the Parisian rooftops, a flicker of defiance ignited within her. She would warn them. She would find a way to reach them, to unite them against this unimaginable threat. She would fight even if it meant facing an impossible adversary in a desolate wasteland, even if it meant confronting her own deepest fears. The gathering storm was upon them, and she would face it head-on. For herself, for her friends, for the world that was on the brink of destruction. The vision was terrifying, but it was also a wake-up call, a catalyst for action. The time for hiding was over. The fight for survival had entered a new, more desperate phase. The war had escalated, and the stakes were higher than ever before.

Marcus's Burning Fury

The Parisian dawn painted the sky in hues of bruised purple and angry orange, a fitting backdrop to the turmoil brewing within Marcus. He hadn't slept, hadn't been able to since the vision – a searing flash of fire, a city consumed by flames, the screams echoing in his mind like a death knell. The vision wasn't a premonition, not exactly. It was more like a warning, a glimpse into a future he could inadvertently create. His pyrokinesis, once a source of terrifying power, now felt like a curse, a volatile beast caged within his very being, threatening to break free and consume everything in its path.

He paced his cramped, dimly lit room, the floorboards groaning under his weight. The air hung heavy with the scent of woodsmoke and sweat, a grim reminder of the relentless training he'd endured under the watchful eyes of the military. Memories, fragmented and brutal, flickered at the edges of his consciousness – the searing pain of the experiments, the cold indifference of his captors, the ever-present fear of failure. He clenched his fists, the knuckles white against his tanned skin, the raw power coiled within him a palpable entity.

The escape had been a blur of adrenaline and chaos, a desperate flight from a life of controlled brutality. He'd found solace in the anonymity of the city, the bustling streets and shadowy alleys providing a semblance of freedom. But freedom, he was discovering, was a fragile thing, a precious illusion easily shattered. The vision had shattered the illusion for him. It had exposed the terrifying potential of his power and the catastrophic consequences of losing control.

He was not a weapon, and he was not a tool. He was a man burdened by an extraordinary gift that threatened to become his undoing. The military had honed his abilities, turning him into a walking inferno. But they hadn't prepared him for the emotional toll, the crushing weight of responsibility that came with such raw power. The memory of his fellow mutants, each marked by their own unique enhancements and enduring their own unique traumas, flashed through his mind; Irina's haunted eyes, Elara's unpredictable storms, Seraphina's psychic anguish – they were all victims of the same twisted experiment, all bearing the scars of the Tempête project. He felt a kinship with them, a bond forged in shared suffering, but the distance was immeasurable, the threat of Thomas a constant, chilling presence.

He reached out a hand, the air shimmering faintly above his palm as he fought to control the growing flames. The heat, the searing energy, pulsed within him, a living fire threatening to consume him. He closed his eyes, focusing on his breathing, attempting to calm the raging storm within. He had to find a way to control this, to master his power before it mastered him before it destroyed everything he held dear. But how could he control something so inherently chaotic, something so intimately tied to his very essence?

The answer, he realized with a jolt, lay not in suppressing the fire but in understanding it, in harnessing its energy rather than fighting it. His past training had been brutal, focusing solely on the destructive potential of his pyrokinesis. He'd been taught to use fire as a weapon, not as a tool. He had to relearn to find a new path, a path of control and precision. It was a monumental task, an enormous effort that demanded immense discipline and an unwavering focus. But the alternative was unthinkable: a future consumed by his own power, a pyre of his own making.

The weight of this responsibility settled heavily upon him. He was not just responsible for himself. He was responsible for preventing the catastrophe he'd seen in his vision. This understanding fueled him, giving him a purpose and a sense of urgency. He spent days scouring libraries and archives, poring over ancient texts, obscure scientific journals, and any source that could give him a better understanding of his abilities. He researched combustion, thermodynamics, and the physics of fire, searching for any clue, any hint that could unlock the secrets of his power. He studied the works of alchemists, delving into their mystical understanding of fire, trying to find a balance between ancient wisdom and modern scientific knowledge. His research became an obsession, his days and nights a blur of activity, fueled by a desperate need to gain control before it was too late.

But knowledge alone wasn't enough. He needed practice, needed to hone his skills, to refine his technique. He sought out secluded locations, abandoned warehouses, and forgotten quarries where he could experiment without risking the lives of innocent bystanders. The training was grueling often painful. He pushed himself to the brink of exhaustion, his body screaming in protest, his mind teetering on the edge of collapse. He learned to channel his power, to shape the flames, to control their intensity, to summon forth small, precisely controlled bursts of fire, then larger, more powerful ones, eventually learning to manipulate the very essence of combustion. He learned to draw upon his internal energy, channeling it through his movements, his body becoming a conduit for the destructive force he carried within.

He was not just fighting against his power, and he was dancing with it, a precarious and dangerous waltz between control and chaos. The process was grueling, filled with setbacks and near-misses. There were times when the fire threatened to overwhelm him when he felt the horrifying sensation of losing control, of being consumed by the very force he sought to master. But each failure was a lesson, each near-catastrophe a step closer to mastery. He learned to temper his rage, to channel his frustration into focus, transforming his fury into a precise, controlled force.

As the weeks turned into months, a transformation took place. The volatile, uncontrolled pyrokinesis began to yield to his disciplined will. He learned to shape the flames into intricate patterns, to summon bursts of fire with surgical precision, and to control the heat and intensity with minute accuracy. His movements became fluid, almost balletic, his body a living expression of his mastery over his power. He was no longer a walking inferno; he was a sculptor of fire, a conductor of raw energy. He was a force to be reckoned with.

But even as he gained control, the vision remained, a constant reminder of the devastating potential of his power. He knew that the threat was not solely external; it was internal as well. The burden of his gift was immense, the weight of responsibility heavier than he could ever have imagined. The gathering storm was still upon them, a storm of his own making, and he knew he would have to face it, not only for his own survival but for the survival of everyone he had sworn to protect. The fight for survival had been a race against time, and he had won, but at what cost? He was a walking weapon, a paradox of destruction and control. The world trembled before Marcus's inner and outer storms as he mastered his power. The true battle, however, was only just beginning. He had to find his fellow mutants, to unite them against the inevitable confrontation with Thomas, a battle that would determine the fate of them all. His journey had just begun.

Chapter 7: Confrontation

The Ambush

The biting Parisian wind whipped around them, carrying the scent of rain and the metallic tang of blood. The abandoned railway yard, shrouded in the pre-dawn gloom, provided little cover. Irina, her usually sharp eyes narrowed, gripped a rusty pipe, its jagged edges mirroring the jagged edges of her own anxiety. Beside her, Elara's face was pale, her hands flickering with barely contained energy, the air around her shimmering with latent power. Marcus, his usually flamboyant attire replaced by somber practicality, stood guard, his fiery aura subdued, a simmering volcano held precariously in check. Seraphina, her senses strained, scanned the shadows, her telepathic tendrils reaching out, searching for any sign of their pursuer.

They had chosen this desolate location for their stand, a place where the city's sprawling indifference offered a semblance of protection. But it was a thin veil. Thomas was relentless, a shadow clinging to their heels for five long years. His enhanced senses, honed to a deadly precision by the military, made him a predator of unparalleled skill. They knew this; they felt it in the chill that seeped into their bones, the way the wind seemed to whisper his name.

The silence was broken only by the distant rumble of a train, a harsh counterpoint to the hushed tension that bound them. Irina glanced at her companions, a silent communication passing between them. This was it. The confrontation they had been dreading, the battle that would determine their fate. Escape was no longer an option; survival was their only goal.

Suddenly, a tremor ran through the ground, subtle but unmistakable. The air crackled with static, and a low growl, almost animalistic in its intensity, echoed from the shadows. Thomas.

He emerged from the darkness, a figure silhouetted against the pale light of the emerging dawn. His movements were fluid, almost balletic in their grace, yet each gesture spoke of lethal intent. His eyes, magnified and sharpened by his enhanced senses, seemed to pierce through them, reading their thoughts, their fears. He was a creature of the night, a phantom given form, a living embodiment of their shared past.

"It ends here," his voice was a low rumble, devoid of emotion, a stark contrast to the storm brewing within them.

Irina stepped forward, her defiance a stark contrast to her fear. "Not while we still breathe, Thomas," she retorted, her voice sharp and clear, cutting through the oppressive silence. "We will not surrender."

Thomas's lips curled into a grim smile. "Your defiance is admirable, Irina. But it's futile. Your escape has been a game of cat and mouse, a desperate bid for freedom. But the game is over."

He advanced, his movements deliberate, his purpose unwavering. Elara reacted instantly, summoning a gust of wind that rocked him, attempting to disrupt his approach. The wind howled around him, but he remained unyielding, his body seemingly impervious to its force. He was more than just a man; he was a weapon, meticulously crafted and honed for destruction.

Marcus, sensing the shift in the dynamics, prepared himself. The air around him shimmered with anticipation, the faintest whisper of fire threatening to erupt. Seraphina, meanwhile, probed Thomas's mind, attempting to read his intentions, to understand his motivations. But Thomas's mind was a fortress, impenetrable to her psychic probes. Years of military conditioning had hardened his psyche, shielding him from external influence.

The battle erupted, a chaotic ballet of power and desperation. Elara unleashed a torrent of rain, turning the yard into a muddy battlefield, her control over the elements a frightening display of raw power. Marcus, his control wavering only slightly, unleashed blasts of fire, forcing Thomas to retreat to dodge the fiery projectiles. Irina, agile and quick, used her knowledge of the terrain to her advantage, using the rusty railway infrastructure to her advantage, exploiting every crack and crevice.

But Thomas was more than a match for them. He moved with an uncanny grace, dodging their attacks with ease, his enhanced reflexes and strength allowing him to overcome their combined assaults. He was a relentless force, pushing forward, his eyes burning with unwavering determination. He moved with a precision that suggested years of brutal training, years spent honing his skills to an almost inhuman level. He moved with the grace of a dancer and the precision of a surgeon.

The fight raged on, a brutal clash of extraordinary powers. Seraphina, trapped between her loyalty to her friends and her growing understanding of Thomas's predicament, experienced the conflict in him – the struggle between duty and conscience. She saw flashes of his training, of the inhuman cruelty he'd witnessed, and the sheer weight of his obedience. Yet, there were other flashes, glimpses of his own internal conflict, his own gnawing doubts.

Suddenly, Irina saw her chance. She launched herself at Thomas, aiming for his exposed side. He turned just in time, the impact throwing her off balance. But in that split second, she saw an opening – a flicker of hesitation, a momentary lapse in his usually perfect defenses. With a desperate cry, she used her body to shield Elara from a devastating blow from Thomas.

The impact sent her sprawling, leaving her unconscious, a sacrifice that bought precious time for her comrades. Elara, enraged by Irina's sacrifice, unleashed the full force of her power, a storm of epic proportions, a whirlwind of wind, rain, and lightning that engulfed the entire yard. The storm raged, a furious storm born from grief and rage, obscuring the battlefield in a maelstrom of chaos.

In the eye of the storm, Marcus stood his ground, his pyrokinesis unleashed, a controlled torrent of fire battling the torrential rain. His power seemed to mirror the storm around them, the fire and water clashing, mimicking the internal conflict that tore within Thomas.

The storm raged for what seemed like an eternity, a terrifying display of raw power. When it finally subsided, leaving behind a landscape transformed, the combatants were scattered, exhausted, wounded, but still alive. The confrontation had reached its climax, but its resolution remained elusive, hanging in the balance like the fragile truce between the storm and the earth. The true cost of their struggle was yet to be counted.

Thomas's Internal Conflict

The ringing silence following the storm's fury was almost more unsettling than the storm itself. Thomas stood amidst the wreckage, his enhanced senses amplifying every creak of twisted metal, every rustle of displaced debris. He felt the lingering thrum of Elara's power, the faint psychic residue of Seraphina's distress, and the residual heat radiating from Marcus's scorched earth. He had done what he was trained to do – hunt them down, subdue them. Yet, the victory felt hollow and bitter. A bitter taste lingered on his tongue, a taste of ash and regret.

He hadn't killed them. He couldn't. Not really. The training had instilled in him an unwavering loyalty, a ruthless efficiency. But somewhere deep within the meticulously constructed soldier, a flicker of humanity remained a spark that the years of conditioning hadn't entirely extinguished. He saw their fear their desperation, felt the raw pain of their injuries, and a strange dissonance resonated within him. It was disharmony between the programmed obedience and the growing empathy that was slowly, relentlessly chipping away at the foundation of his being.

He remembered the days before the conditioning, the fleeting moments of friendship shared in the secret laboratories of Tempête, and the shared anxieties and hopes before the military's intrusion. He recalled Irina's brilliance, her mind a labyrinth of possibilities, her laughter like wind chimes in a summer breeze. Elara, with her playful spirit and her capacity for both creation and destruction, was a force of nature, a whirlwind of emotion and power. Marcus, with his passionate heart and unpredictable outbursts, was a force that was both exhilarating and terrifying. Even Seraphina, with her quiet intensity her piercing insight into the hearts and minds of others, commanded a respect that went beyond fear.

These weren't mere targets; they were individuals, flawed and vibrant, just like him. The realization struck him with the force of a physical blow, shattering the carefully constructed walls of his programmed loyalty. He had hunted them, pursued them relentlessly, driven by a blind obedience that now seemed monstrously cruel.

The years of relentless pursuit had taken a toll. The constant pressure, the relentless hunt, had worn him down. He was exhausted, not just physically but emotionally. The weight of his actions, the burden of his existence, pressed down on him like a physical weight. Each successful capture, each near-miss, each harrowing confrontation had chipped away at his soul, leaving behind a void filled with self-doubt and a gnawing sense of profound guilt.

He looked at his hands, still stained with the grime of the battle, still capable of inflicting unimaginable damage. But they also possessed the ability to heal, to mend, to soothe. This duality was his own internal conflict, a constant tug-of-war between destruction and creation, between obedience and empathy. He was a weapon, a tool, a product of scientific ambition gone horribly wrong. But he was also something more, something that defied the cold logic that had created him. He was capable of compassion, of remorse, of love.

His training had emphasized efficiency, ruthlessness, and unwavering loyalty. Any sign of hesitation, any display of empathy, was met with harsh punishment, designed to break down resistance and instill absolute obedience. But the very act of hunting his former comrades, of seeing their fear, their pain, their resilience, had awakened a slumbering conscience. He saw reflections of himself in their struggles, their defiance in the face of insurmountable odds. They were fighting for survival, for their very existence, just as he, in a strange, twisted way, was fighting to reclaim his own humanity.

The memory-erasing serum, the whispers he'd overheard about its creation, and Dr. Reed's continued work added another layer to his internal conflict. Could he, should he, seek them out? Could he use his own enhanced senses and abilities to find them and ensure their safety, thereby betraying the military's trust? The thought was both terrifying and exhilarating. He was trained to kill, but could he choose to save?

The wind howled a mournful cry through the skeletal remains of the railway yard, mirroring the turmoil within him. He was caught in a moral quagmire, a battleground where loyalty clashed with conscience. Obedience warred with empathy. He was a creature of science, a product of ambition and manipulation, yet he possessed the capacity for choice, for rebellion, for redemption. The future hung in the balance, as uncertain and unpredictable as the storm that had just raged around him.

The weight of his actions pressed heavily upon him. He had followed orders, obeyed his programming, and hunted his former comrades with ruthless efficiency. But he hadn't killed them. He couldn't bring himself to do it. There were moments during the confrontation where he'd hesitated, moments where the ingrained training faltered, moments where his enhanced senses picked up on the fear and desperation radiating from Irina, Elara, Marcus, and Seraphina. These moments, these brief cracks in his programmed facade, had planted the seeds of doubt, fostering the beginnings of a conscience he never knew he possessed.

He knew the implications of his actions, or rather, his inaction. He had betrayed the trust placed in him by the military. He was a rogue element, a loose cannon, a danger to both sides of the conflict. Yet, the alternative – the cold, calculated extermination of his former colleagues – was unthinkable. The moral cost was too high.

His enhanced senses were a curse and a blessing. They amplified the horrors of the battlefield, the sounds of agony, the scent of blood, the raw terror emanating from his opponents, and his own guilt and self-loathing. They also honed his awareness of the environment, his ability to predict his enemies' moves, and his capacity to escape unscathed, allowing him to delay the inevitable confrontation.

But the delay was not a solution. It was merely postponing the inevitable decision he had to make. The military would relentlessly pursue him, demanding answers demanding results. Tempête, too, would become aware of his reluctance to eradicate his former associates. He was trapped in a web of deceit and betrayal, with no easy escape.

He thought about the serum, the memory-erasing concoction developed by Tempête. It represented a potential escape route, not just for his former colleagues but for himself. To erase his memories, to erase the horrors he'd witnessed, the horrors he'd inflicted, to erase his past and start anew. But could he truly escape his past? Could he erase the memories and feelings that were already forever etched onto his soul? Was that truly freedom or simply a form of self-deception?

The choice was a profound one, a moral crossroads where his very existence hung in the balance. To remain loyal to his programming, to continue the hunt, to obey the commands ingrained within him, or to rebel, to defy the system that had created him, to choose empathy over obedience, to embrace the humanity he'd been so diligently trained to suppress. He was caught between two worlds, two identities, and two conflicting loyalties.

The wind continued to howl, a mournful symphony of uncertainty and doubt. The darkness pressed in, a tangible entity mirroring the moral darkness within him. The dawn was approaching, promising a new day, but Thomas was unsure if he could ever truly face the light. He was a paradox, a contradiction, a weapon capable of both destruction and healing, a creature of science caught in a moral labyrinth of his own making. And the answer to his internal conflict, to the choice he had to make, remained elusive, shrouded in the shadows of the Parisian dawn.

Irina's Sacrifice

The Parisian dawn painted the sky in hues of bruised purple and angry orange, a fitting backdrop to the wreckage of the previous night's battle. Thomas, his senses still reeling from the confrontation, found himself drawn to a hidden alleyway, its entrance obscured by a crumpled billboard advertising a long-forgotten perfume. He'd sensed a faint flicker of… something. Not the raw power of Elara or Marcus, but something more subtle, a whisper of intellect, fading rapidly.

He pushed aside the debris, the metallic tang of blood heavy in the air. Irina lay huddled against a cold brick wall, a single, shallow breath escaping her lips. Her usually vibrant eyes, pools of sharp intelligence, were clouded with an unnatural stillness. A small, almost imperceptible device pulsed faintly against her temple, its rhythmic thrum a stark counterpoint to the silence of the alley.

"Irina?" he whispered, his voice rough with a mixture of concern and something akin to guilt. He knelt beside her, his enhanced hearing picking up the faint, irregular beat of her heart, a drumbeat against the looming silence. The device, a small, intricately crafted piece of technology, was unlike anything he'd encountered before. Its surface was cool to the touch, yet it seemed to radiate a chilling energy.

He carefully examined the device, his enhanced senses struggling to penetrate its protective shielding. It wasn't a weapon, not in the traditional sense. It was… a data transfer device of a sophistication he hadn't believed possible. It was draining her, systematically transferring the immense data contained within her super-intelligent mind. He recognized the signature of Tempete's research—a desperate attempt to salvage their work, to preserve the fruits of their forbidden experiments.

The realization hit him with the force of a physical blow. Irina hadn't been defeated in battle; she had been… sacrificed. A sacrifice to preserve the knowledge that the military, or perhaps some other, even more sinister entity, craved. The device wasn't just draining her intelligence. It was stealing her very essence, leaving her a hollow shell.

His fingers brushed against her forehead, feeling the chilling coldness of the device pressed against her skin. He could feel the agonizing process, the relentless drain on her mental capabilities, the systematic eradication of her unique consciousness. He was trained to kill, to subdue, but this… this was different. This was a slow, torturous murder. A calculated theft.

Anger, raw and violent, coursed through him. He wasn't sure who had done this – the military, some rival organization, or even Tempête themselves in a desperate act of self-preservation. It didn't matter. His training, the years of conditioning, were momentarily eclipsed by a surge of primal rage. He wanted vengeance. He would find those responsible, no matter the cost.

But there was also a deeper emotion, a gnawing guilt, a silent scream of regret. He had hunted these people, his own kind, his former colleagues, driven by cold obedience he could no longer justify. He was their executioner, a weapon that had been used to silence them one by one. Now, seeing Irina in this state, a testament to the brutal cruelty of this project, the full weight of his actions crashed down upon him.

He looked around the alleyway, his senses strained, searching for any clue, any trace of the perpetrators. The device was far too advanced to be deactivated without specialized knowledge. He knew he needed help, someone with the expertise to stop the process and, perhaps, save Irina. But who could he trust? Tempête was scattered, its members either dead or in hiding. And the people who could help him were those same people who had created this horrific weapon in the first place.

He gently lifted Irina, careful to avoid jarring the device. She felt impossibly light, her body devoid of the vibrant energy he remembered. He carried her through the rubble-strewn streets of Paris, the city's morning sounds muffled, distant, unreal. He needed to reach Dubois, Moreau, or Petrova. They were the only ones who might understand this technology and might have a chance to reverse the process to save his friend. But would they even want to? Their involvement in the project and the blood on their hands remained a chilling reminder of the moral doubts about their scientific pursuit.

As he navigated the labyrinthine streets, the memories of his past flooded back – the grueling training, the relentless pursuit, the crushing weight of his mission. He'd been a tool, a weapon, blindly following orders, a soldier in a war he never understood. Now, staring at Irina's lifeless form, he understood the true cost of that obedience. The price of unchecked scientific ambition. The moral bankruptcy of those who created weapons of such terrifying power.

He recalled the nights spent studying Irina's brilliant mind, her capacity for learning, and her extraordinary intellect. Her ability to process information at speeds that defied comprehension. Now, that brilliance was being cruelly stolen, replaced by an empty void. He remembered her laughter, her wit, her unwavering loyalty to those she cared for. And the realization that she had sacrificed herself for the rest of them, a silent act of courage and love.

He reached the abandoned laboratory, a crumbling testament to Tempete's twisted ambitions. He found Dubois, his face etched with the weariness of a man haunted by his past. The doctor's eyes widened when he saw Irina, her frail body suspended in his arms. He recognized the device instantly, a shudder running through his frame. He had designed it, hadn't he? A tool for preservation, a means to save their legacy. But at what cost?

"It's draining her," Thomas said, his voice hoarse with exhaustion and despair. "It's taking everything."

Dubois nodded, his gaze fixed on the device. His own face mirrored the agony he had no doubt been experiencing for years, watching the consequences of their actions unfold. The years of relentless research, the impossible breakthroughs, the unwavering belief in their cause – now all reduced to this horrific scene. He looked at Irina, a ghost of his former brilliance, a victim of his own ambition.

He worked frantically, his hands moving with a speed and precision born from years of experience. The air crackled with energy as he connected various wires and devices, attempting to counter the drain. The process was delicate and perilous. One wrong move, and Irina would be lost forever.

Hours crawled by, each moment filled with agonizing tension. Dubois's brow was beaded with sweat, his face pale with exertion. Thomas watched, his heart a captive bird in his chest. He felt the weight of Irina's sacrifice, the gravity of their shared past, and the heavy burden of his future. This wasn't just about saving a life; it was about redemption, about confronting the ghosts of his past and finally accepting the responsibility for his actions.

As the dawn broke again, painting the sky with a new palette of hope, Dubois stepped back, his breath ragged. The device fell silent. Irina's breathing, though shallow, had stabilized. The color had slowly started to return to her cheeks, a faint blush replacing the deathly pallor.

The rescue was far from over. Irina's mind might be intact, but the long process of recovery loomed ahead, fraught with uncertainty. Yet, as he looked at Irina's pale face, he saw a flicker of recognition, a spark of intelligence rekindled from the brink of oblivion. A silent promise of life, a tenuous thread of hope in the aftermath of a devastating sacrifice. The battle had been won, but the war was far from over. And Thomas knew, with a chilling certainty, that this victory came at an immeasurable cost. The shadows of Tempete's legacy stretched long and dark, a reminder of the dangerous intersection between scientific ambition and moral compromise.

Elara's Climactic Storm

The air crackled with anticipation, a tangible tension hanging heavier than the Parisian smog. Thomas crouched low behind a crumbling fountain, his enhanced senses screaming warnings, and felt the shift before he saw it. A tremor, subtle at first, like the earth itself taking a shuddering breath. Then, the wind. It whipped around him, a frantic, icy hand clawing at his clothes, tossing debris into a chaotic dance. The sky, moments ago a bruised purple, was now a roiling canvas of black and bruised grey, the clouds churning like a malevolent beast roused from its slumber.

This wasn't a natural storm. This was Elara.

He'd felt her presence before, a distant whisper of raw power, but this… this was a frenzy of controlled fury, a storm deliberately unleashed. The rain began, not as gentle drops, but as a torrential downpour, each drop a miniature projectile slamming against the cobblestones. The wind howled a mournful symphony of destruction, tearing at the weakened structures of the city. Cars overturned; the storm's roar swallowed their metallic shrieks. The scent of ozone filled the air, sharp and harsh, burning the back of his throat.

Thomas felt a flicker of admiration tinged with a chilling dread. Elara wasn't just powerful; she was precise. This storm wasn't random chaos; it was strategically aimed, a weaponized storm designed to overwhelm and crush. He could almost feel her intent, a fierce, desperate will to protect herself and, perhaps, her remaining comrades.

The military escort, a group of heavily armed soldiers equipped with specialized weather-resistant gear, struggled against the onslaught. Their efforts were futile. The storm was too powerful, too relentless. The soldiers fought to maintain their footing, and their vehicles rocked like toys in a bathtub. Their weapons, designed for conventional warfare, were useless against the sheer force of nature Elara commanded. Lightning cracked, illuminating the scene in flashes of blinding white, each bolt a precise, terrifying strike targeted at their positions. The soldiers screamed, the sound swallowed by the wind's fury.

Thomas saw a flash of movement in the periphery, a fleeting glimpse of a soldier separated from his unit, thrown against a wall by a rogue gust of wind. The man lay still, a broken marionette in the storm's cruel dance. A surge of guilt, unexpected and sharp, pierced Thomas. He was a hunter, trained to kill, but this… this wasn't a fair fight. This was annihilation.

The military's relentless pursuit, their disregard for human life, was starting to weigh heavily on him. The lines between hunter and hunted, between right and wrong, were blurring. The memory of Irina's near-death experience the fragility of her survival, reinforced his growing unease. He'd almost lost her, another casualty in this senseless war. The cost was too high.

The storm intensified, the wind a screaming banshee tearing through the city. Buildings groaned under the strain, their windows shattering like fragile glass. The rain was now mixed with hail, each icy pellet a stinging blow. Thomas sought shelter behind a toppled statue, the cold rain soaking him to the bone. His enhanced senses were overwhelmed, the harshness of the storm a deafening assault on his heightened perception.

He wondered if Elara was aware of his presence, if she intended for him to witness her power, to feel the weight of her despair. Or perhaps, her rage. The storm felt less like a desperate attempt to survive and more like an act of vengeful defiance. It was as if she had unleashed not only the power of nature but also her own suppressed fury, a pent-up energy unleashed upon the world that had wronged her.

As the storm raged, Thomas felt a strange connection to Elara, a kinship forged in shared trauma and persecution. Both victims of Tempete's experiments had been transformed, manipulated, and forced to fight for a cause they didn't believe in. Yet, she fought with a ferocity he could scarcely comprehend, a raw, untamed power.

He watched helplessly as the storm gradually subsided. The wind died down, replaced by the gentle patter of rain. The clouds parted, revealing a sky that was oddly calm and serene. The scene that unfolded before him was one of devastation. The once-proud city was marred with destruction, a testament to Elara's rage. The military soldiers were scattered, wounded, and thoroughly defeated. The once-organized ranks were now a collection of battered figures struggling to comprehend the scale of the destruction they'd encountered.

But Elara was gone. Vanished without a trace, leaving behind only the wreckage of her fury and the echo of her power. Thomas, soaked to the bone and emotionally drained, knew that this confrontation had changed him. He couldn't ignore the moral implications of his actions, the horrifying cost of the military's obsession with enhanced individuals.

The hunt continued, but it was no longer a simple matter of capture and containment. The lines had blurred beyond recognition. He was no longer just a soldier following orders but a man haunted by the consequences of unchecked scientific ambition, a man grappling with the ethical complexities of a world irrevocably altered by Tempete's legacy. The whispers of the past, the memories of his friends, both dead and alive, echoed in his ears, fueling a growing rebellion within him.

The storm had passed, but its aftermath was far from over. The city lay broken, mirroring the fractured state of his own soul. He knew that the true confrontation was yet to come, a battle not fought with weapons or weather but with the very conscience of a man caught between loyalty and rebellion, obedience and freedom. He had to find a way to end this war, even if it meant defying those who had trained him, those who held the reins of power. The cost of silence, he realized, was far greater than any risk he was willing to take. The whispers of his conscience were now louder than any order, stronger than any command. The battle had moved beyond the battlefield into the depths of his own soul. And he knew, with unwavering certainty, that he had to choose a side. A side that perhaps meant betraying everything he once believed in. The future, once clear, was now a chaotic storm of its own.

Marcus's Controlled Fury

The cobblestones, slick with rain and the residue of the storm Elara had unleashed, reflected the flickering gaslight. Thomas stood poised, his enhanced senses straining to pierce the gloom, his breath misting in the frigid air. He had expected Irina's sharp intellect to anticipate his move, to lay traps, to create a maze of deadly diversions. He'd even prepared for Seraphina's insidious whispers, the mind-bending onslaught that could shatter a man's resolve. But Marcus... Marcus was a different beast altogether. The raw, untamed power he wielded was terrifying in its potential, a volatile force that could consume the city in a fiery inferno.

Thomas had tracked him to a derelict warehouse district, the air thick with the stench of decay and damp earth. The building itself seemed to groan under the weight of years of neglect, a skeletal frame against the bruised twilight sky. He heard it before he saw it – a low hum, a barely perceptible vibration that resonated deep within his bones. The hum intensified, growing into a deep, resonant thrum like the heartbeat of some slumbering giant. Then, a flicker. A single, dancing ember, growing rapidly into a blazing inferno that burst forth from a shattered window.

Marcus stood silhouetted against the raging flames, a dark figure amidst a vortex of fire and smoke. He wasn't the crazed, uncontrolled pyromancer Thomas remembered from their training days. This Marcus was different. This Marcus was calculating precise, his movements efficient and deliberate. He controlled the flames, shaping them, molding them to his will like a sculptor working with clay. The fire didn't engulf the entire warehouse; instead, it danced in carefully choreographed patterns, creating walls of searing heat and curtains of fire that blocked off escape routes.

Thomas knew he couldn't fight fire with fire; his enhanced senses, his healing abilities, would be useless against such overwhelming power. He needed strategy, cunning, a way to exploit the limits of Marcus's control, however finely honed. He needed to remind Marcus of the humanity beneath the pyrokinetic abilities to reach the man who had once been his comrade, lost in the shadow of fear and resentment.

He advanced cautiously, moving through the ruins of the warehouse district, the air growing hotter with each step. He spotted a narrow alleyway, a potential flanking maneuver, but the walls themselves seemed to breathe with heat, radiating a tangible force that would scorch him if he dared to touch them. Marcus was anticipating his every move, a deadly game of cat and mouse played in the heart of a burning city.

The smell of burning wood and singed flesh reached Thomas's nostrils. He could feel the heat on his face, a searing wave that threatened to overwhelm his senses. But he pressed on, the memory of his past, the horrors of the military's training, fueling his determination. He had to find a way to reach Marcus, to break through the wall of fire and controlled fury that separated them.

He saw it then, a small detail easily missed amidst the chaos. A section of the warehouse's exterior wall, weakened by years of neglect and now further compromised by the intense heat, was starting to crumble. A small crack, widening slowly but surely. This was his opportunity.

Thomas moved with the grace of a predator, his movements fluid and silent. He avoided the direct flames, using the shadows and the crumbling debris as cover. He approached the weakening wall, its bricks glowing with intense heat. He reached the crack and, with a sudden, powerful shove, dislodged a large section of the wall, causing it to collapse into the inferno within.

The resulting explosion of fire and debris was momentarily blinding, a chaotic wave of heat and destruction. But amidst the chaos, Thomas saw Marcus flinch, the calculated precision of his control faltering for a fraction of a second. That fraction was all Thomas needed.

He seized the opportunity, yelling a name, not a command, not an order, but a word from their shared past, a memory from a time before the experiments, before the military, before the brutal training. A single word that cut through the fire, the fury, the decades of separation.

"Dmitri?"

The name, spoken in a voice raw with emotion, resonated in the air, a stark counterpoint to the crackling flames. Marcus froze his control over the pyrokinesis, visibly wavering. The flames dimmed, their ferocious dance slowing, the inferno subsiding. The raw power that had threatened to consume the city began to recede, replaced by a hesitant, flickering glow.

The ensuing silence was heavy and thick with unspoken words and unresolved emotions. The fire had subsided, but the true battle was just beginning – a battle not of fire and fury but of memory and conscience, of shared trauma and the possibility of redemption. The fight was far from over, but in the heart of the ravaged warehouse, a fragile bridge had been built, a connection forged between two men fractured by war, scarred by the past, and desperate for a future beyond the reach of the shadows.

The air cleared slightly, the smoke beginning to dissipate, revealing the extent of the damage. The warehouse was a smoldering ruin, a testament to the power Marcus wielded but also a testament to his newfound capacity for restraint, a sign of the battle he fought within himself. Thomas stepped forward, approaching Marcus slowly, cautiously. He saw a flicker of something in Marcus's eyes – a glimmer of the man he once knew, the man buried beneath years of pain, fear, and obedience.

This was not the end but a fragile beginning, a glimmer of hope in the ashes of a broken city. The weight of their shared history pressed down heavily on them, the memories of Tempête, the brutal military training, and the years of hunting and being hunted all merging into a heavy silence. Thomas knew this was only the first step in a long, arduous journey toward healing and reconciliation, a journey filled with uncertainty, with the constant threat of relapse, but a journey that had to be undertaken, a path they had to cross together if they were to escape the shadows that had held them captive for so long. The future remained uncertain, a dark tapestry woven with threads of hope and despair, but for the first time in a long time, both men felt a flicker of something approaching peace. A hard-won peace, born amidst the ashes of their shared past. A fragile peace that could shatter at any moment, but a peace nonetheless.

The city, scarred but not broken, stood as a silent witness to the confrontation, to the battle fought not only between two men but within their hearts, a battle that could determine not only their futures but the fate of those who had once been their comrades, those who still remained at large, haunted by the legacy of Tempête. The silence hung heavy, eager with the weight of unspoken words, the burden of shared trauma, the possibility of forgiveness, and the daunting task of rebuilding a life shattered by science's relentless pursuit of power. This power had unleashed chaos and destruction, leaving behind a trail of broken lives and unresolved conflicts. And in the heart of that ruin, under a sky that was slowly beginning to clear, two men stood, facing a future that was as unpredictable and volatile as the flames that had danced between them.

Chapter 8: Revelations

Uncovering The Truth

The biting Parisian wind whipped around Irina, stinging her cheeks as she huddled deeper into the shadows of the abandoned railway yard. Five years since the escape, five years since she'd last seen Elara's face, felt Seraphina's calming touch or witnessed Marcus's controlled inferno. Five years since Thomas, the weapon they'd all once been, had become their relentless hunter. But tonight, something felt different. A tremor of anticipation, laced with a chilling premonition, ran through her. A coded message, delivered by a fleeting contact, spoke of a meeting, a revelation. The location: an old, disused laboratory not far from the very place where their nightmare had begun.

The laboratory was a crumbling husk, the stench of decay and damp earth clinging to the air. Inside, flickering gaslights cast long, distorted shadows, revealing peeling paint and rusted equipment. The others were already there, their faces etched with a mixture of apprehension and hope. Elara, her eyes mirroring the storm clouds gathering outside, her hands nervously fiddling with a small, intricate device. Seraphina, her usual calm replaced by a palpable tension, her eyes closed as if listening to something beyond the tangible world. And Marcus, his usual volatile energy subdued, a smoldering ember in the darkness.

Irina joined them, her eyes scanning the room for any sign of danger. The air crackled with an unspoken question, a shared anxiety that hung heavier than the dust motes dancing in the weak light. Then, from the shadows, a figure emerged. Not Thomas, but someone else. A wizened old man, his face etched with the lines of years and secrets, his eyes holding a depth of knowledge that sent a shiver down Irina's spine. He was Dr. Armand Dubois, one of the original scientists of Tempête, a man they believed to have erased his memories with the serum five years ago.

"You received the message," Dubois rasped, his voice barely a whisper. "Good. There's much to explain, much that you need to know."

He began to speak, his words painting a picture far darker and more insidious than anything they could have imagined. Tempête, it turned out, hadn't been simply about curing consumption. The original goal, he revealed, had been far more ambitious, far more sinister. The consumption research had been a cover, a smokescreen for a deeper project – a project aimed at creating a new breed of super soldier, not just for the French military, but for a far more powerful, far more shadowy organization. An organization that stretched its tendrils across the globe, its influence reaching the highest echelons of power.

The organization, Dubois explained, wasn't simply weaponizing the mutants. They were interested in something far more profound – controlling the very fabric of reality. The enhanced abilities weren't merely a side effect of the genetic manipulation; they were the key to unlocking something far more powerful, something they called "The Convergence." The Convergence, he explained, was a point in time where the boundaries between dimensions blurred, a point where reality itself could be altered. And the mutants, with their amplified abilities, were the key to accessing it.

"They believed," Dubois continued, his voice laced with bitter regret, "that by controlling you, by harnessing your powers, they could manipulate reality itself. They could rewrite history and reshape the future. They saw you not as weapons but as gods."

His words hung heavy in the air, the enormity of the revelation settling upon them like a shroud. The military's involvement, the brutal training, the relentless pursuit – all of it had been a pawn in a far larger game, a game played by unseen hands, with the mutants as their unwitting pieces. The weight of this realization was almost unbearable.

Elara, her face pale, spoke her voice barely a tremor. "And Thomas... he was part of it all along?"

Dubois nodded, a single tear tracing a path through the wrinkles on his weathered face. "He was their most successful creation, the perfect instrument. Conditioned to obey, incapable of dissent. But..." he paused, his gaze meeting Irina's, "even the most perfectly crafted weapon can break."

The revelation about Thomas wasn't merely that he had been a pawn. It was that his unwavering loyalty his ruthless efficiency had been the result of a sophisticated form of mind control, far more advanced than anything they had previously suspected. The conditioning had been so thorough, so complete, that even his own moral compass had been overwritten.

The conversation then turned to the memory-erasing serum. The scientists hadn't fully understood its effects, Dubois admitted. While it effectively erased memories of Tempete's work, it hadn't completely eradicated the underlying psychological conditioning. He speculated that elements of their original programming still lingered, dormant, perhaps even waiting to be awakened. This meant the remaining scientists, including Dr. Reed, might be more susceptible to manipulation than they had previously thought. It cast a chilling light on Reed's continued involvement, raising uncomfortable questions about his loyalty and motivations.

The serum, Dubois went on to explain, was far from a simple memory eraser. It also contained elements designed to suppress the mutants' abilities, a detail they had only recently discovered. The organization, fearing the full potential of their creations, had added this component as a safeguard, a failsafe to prevent the mutants from ever reaching their full power. This explained why, despite their enhanced capabilities, they had struggled to maintain control over their powers and why they had been susceptible to the organization's control for so long.

The final piece of the puzzle was Dr. Reed. Dubois revealed that Reed had known about the true objectives of the organization from the very beginning, even actively participating in the darker aspects of their research. His supposed faith in their work had been a façade, a deliberate act of deception. Reed hadn't abandoned the project; he had remained, manipulating events from the shadows, always one step ahead, always ensuring the organization's interests were served.

The weight of these revelations hung heavily in the air. The escape, the pursuit, the years of struggle – it had all been a carefully orchestrated dance, a game played by masters of manipulation. But the revelation of the truth had also been a turning point. It was a stark reminder that the fight was far from over and that the true enemy was far more powerful, far more insidious than they had ever imagined. The mutants, armed with this knowledge, were faced with a new challenge: to not only survive but to fight back against a force that sought to control the very fabric of reality. The fight for their freedom, their very existence, was just beginning. The future once shrouded in fear and uncertainty, now held the potential for a dangerous, and perhaps glorious, rebellion. The echoes of Tempête, once a whisper in the shadows, were about to become a roar.

Thomas's Betrayal

The biting wind seemed to mock Thomas's enhanced senses, a constant, irritating whisper against the heightened acuity he possessed. He stood atop the Notre Dame Cathedral, the gargoyles his silent sentinels, surveying the city spread out below like a meticulously crafted map. Five years he'd spent as the military's instrument of destruction, a perfectly honed weapon, his every move guided by their cold, calculating directives. Five years of hunting his former colleagues, of feeling the chilling satisfaction of tracking them, of tasting the metallic tang of blood in his mouth after each encounter. But the satisfaction was hollow, a bitter aftertaste on a poisoned tongue.

The memory-erasing serum – a cruel irony, considering the enhancements they'd given him – had become a symbol. He'd seen the blankness in the eyes of the doctors, their amnesia a testament to the horrors they'd unleashed upon the world. Yet, their oblivion hadn't erased the truth from his own heightened senses. He had witnessed the sheer desperation in their eyes during those final nights. They were not villains. They were merely scientists grappling with the consequences of their ambition. And in their fear, a seed of doubt had taken root within him, growing slowly, silently, until it blossomed into a rebellion against his programmed obedience.

The coded message, a faint tremor in the wind, had been his turning point. Irina, ever the strategist, had managed to slip a message to him, a message not directed to the soldier they'd created but to the man beneath the conditioning. It spoke of a meeting, a chance to discuss the larger threat they all faced – the threat that extended far beyond the military's grasp. It was a message hinting at a power more ancient, more insidious than even the Tempête project itself. The message contained a single, chilling phrase: "They are not done with us."

He descended from the cathedral, the city's lights a shimmering tapestry below. He moved with the grace of a predator, his heightened senses guiding him through the labyrinthine streets. His movements were swift and silent, each step measured and calculating. He was still a weapon, but his target had shifted. He wasn't hunting the remnants of Tempête anymore. He was hunting something else.

The old laboratory, a dilapidated shell of its former glory, felt like a tomb. The air inside was thick with the scent of dust, decay, and a faint, lingering metallic tang—the ghost of scientific experimentation. He found them gathered in the shadows, the flickering gaslight casting elongated, distorted shadows on the walls. Irina, her eyes sharp and intelligent, her gaze betraying the years of hardship and unwavering determination. Elara, her aura subtly shifting the temperature in the room, her weather manipulation skills still refined and potent. Seraphina, her face serene yet watchful, her telepathic abilities creating an intense atmosphere of quiet tension. And Marcus, his hands still radiating a subdued heat, a testament to the volatile power he held within.

The reunion was silent, charged with years of unspoken words, shared trauma, bitter resentment, and dawning hope. He looked at their faces, at the resilience etched into their features, and for the first time since his conditioning, he saw them not as targets but as fellow survivors. He had hunted them, and yet they looked at him not with hatred but with a mixture of fear and hope.

"They tried to erase our memories," Irina's voice was low, a whisper in the cavernous space, "but they failed. Some things are too deeply ingrained."

Elara nodded a silent agreement. The serum had failed to erase the core of their experiences, the primal fear, the brutal training, the shared history. The military's attempt to control them had backfired. The memories, though fragmented, had become a catalyst, forging an unbreakable bond between them.

Marcus, ever the volatile one, spoke. "They wanted us to be weapons. But we are something more."

Seraphina's telepathic abilities were subtle, painting vivid images in his mind – fragmented memories of her witnessing the experiments, the cruelty, the brutality. It revealed her true fear and resolve.

"They're after more than just us," Irina continued, her eyes fixed on Thomas. "They're after… something else. Something far more powerful." She revealed the information gleaned from her network of contacts, information about a secret government project seeking to harness and control the very forces that had given them their abilities. It was a project far grander, far more sinister than Tempête. This was not merely about weaponizing mutants; it was about manipulating the fabric of reality itself.

Thomas, despite his conditioning, felt a surge of anger. The rage wasn't directed at his former colleagues; it was targeted at the true architects of this terrifying conspiracy – the ones who had manipulated him, used him, and discarded him as a mere instrument. He listened intently, the revelations chipping away at the last vestiges of his programming, revealing a larger, more terrifying threat than he could have ever imagined.

The revelation had a profound effect. The years of hunting the cold precision of his actions they were all a part of a grand scheme, a carefully orchestrated dance designed to keep him isolated, to prevent him from realizing the larger plot.

He felt the shackles of his conditioning begin to break. He was not simply a weapon; he was a man, and he was making a choice. He looked at his former comrades, their faces filled with a mixture of fear and defiance.

He spoke, his voice hoarse yet filled with a newfound resolve, "I'm with you." His betrayal of the military wasn't a sudden act of rebellion; it was a culmination of years of subtle rebellion, a slow awakening from a state of enforced obedience. It was the realization that his true allegiance wasn't to the men who had created him but to the people who were truly his own kind.

The air crackled with unspoken energy, a sense of fragile hope amidst the overwhelming odds. They were outcasts, mutants, and hunted creatures. But they were together, and in their unity, they found strength, a terrifying and magnificent strength that would soon shake the very foundations of the world. The war had just begun. The fight was far from over, but now they fought not for survival alone but for the chance to determine their own destiny, to rewrite their story, and to face the true enemy, armed with newfound knowledge and a shared purpose. Their next move had to be calculated, precise, and, above all, lethal. The weight of the world rested on their shoulders, and the shadows of Tempete's legacy stretched far into the future, promising both destruction and the glimmer of a revolutionary hope. The betrayal was complete. The hunt had turned into a revolution.

Reed's Manipulation

The Parisian dawn painted the sky in hues of bruised purple and angry orange, mirroring the turmoil brewing within Thomas. He'd met with Irina, Elara, and Seraphina – a secret rendezvous in the catacombs beneath the city. Marcus, ever the volatile force, remained elusive, his fiery temperament making him a risk. They had shared information, piecing together the fragmented memories of their past, the horrifying experiments, the brutal training. But a nagging question remained, a shadow lurking at the edges of their newfound alliance: Dr. Reed.

He was a ghost, a phantom pulling the strings from the darkness. While Drs. Dubois, Moreau, Petrova, and Thorne had sought oblivion in the memory-erasing serum, Reed had remained, a testament to an unsettling dedication. His motives were shrouded in mystery, a puzzle box with only the most terrifying answers staring back from the shadows of its depths. But Irina, with her unparalleled intellect, had begun to unravel the threads of Reed's maneuvers.

"He didn't just oversee the project," Irina said, her voice low, her eyes burning with a cold intensity that was far more chilling than any pyrokinetic flame. "He manipulated it. He guided the military's demands, subtly shaping their objectives. He ensured the serum's creation, a tool to erase the inconvenient truth of the guilt of his partners. He was planning for this. All of it."

The others exchanged uneasy glances. The idea was unsettling – the thought that their suffering had been a carefully orchestrated performance, a macabre puppet show directed by a man they had once trusted. It shattered the fragile unity they had built, sowing the seeds of doubt and suspicion. Thomas, particularly, felt the sting of betrayal. He had been the instrument of Reed's design for five years, his loyalty a carefully constructed weapon.

Irina continued, tracing a pattern on the damp stone wall of the catacombs with her finger. "The military wanted weapons. Reed wanted… something more. Something far more sinister."

Seraphina, her telepathic abilities heightened in the confined space, picked up on a faint echo of thought – a distorted fragment from the past, a chilling whisper of ambition. "He spoke of… evolution. Of transcending humanity. Of creating a new order, a superior race."

The air grew heavy with the weight of their realization. Reed's obsession wasn't merely about scientific advancement; it was about power, about control, about reshaping the very fabric of existence itself. The horrifying implication hung heavy over them - their existence was part of a far grander, more terrifying design than they had ever imagined.

Elara, her mastery of the elements reflecting the storm gathering within their fragile alliance, spoke. "The serum… it wasn't just to erase memories. He used it to control. To manipulate. To shape the outcome of his experiments, ensuring only the most obedient, the most pliable, survived."

This new revelation was a chilling confirmation. The escapees – Irina, Elara, Seraphina, and Marcus – had all shown independent thought, signs of rebellion against Tempête and the military. Those who didn't… they were gone, their fates unknown, their memories erased. Thomas's hunt had been a selective cleansing, leaving only the ones who posed no further threat to Reed's agenda. The horror of it was almost too much to bear.

Their conversation lasted long into the night, the echoes of their discussion bouncing off the ancient stones. They delved deeper into Irina's findings – meticulously compiled data gleaned from stolen military files, cryptic notes, and fragmented memories – revealing a pattern of manipulation so intricate it was both terrifying and awe-inspiring in its scope. Reed had not only shaped the direction of Tempête, but he had also manipulated the flow of information, misleading the military and creating a smokescreen around his true objectives. He had played them all, from his fellow scientists to the power brokers of the military, like pawns in a grand game of chess, a dangerous chess game with humanity as the stakes.

The implications were staggering. Reed's ultimate goal wasn't just to create super-powered individuals; it was to create an army, a loyal army – an army entirely under his control, an army obedient to his vision of a new world order. His ambition was not mere scientific curiosity; it was a megalomaniacal pursuit of power so terrifying it transcended any ethical boundaries. The memory-erasing serum was only one component of this chilling plan. There were other strands to this plot, other elements that were slowly coming into focus.

Thomas, burdened by the weight of his past actions, felt a surge of cold fury. He had been a pawn, a tool, a murderer for a man who viewed humanity as a raw material to be shaped and molded. The realization shook him to his core. His enhanced senses, once his greatest assets, now felt like a curse, amplifying the gnawing guilt and self-loathing. The hunt had been an act of blind obedience; the revolution would be an act of righteous retribution.

The following days were spent planning. Irina devised a plan to infiltrate Reed's hidden laboratory. They needed to discover the extent of his work, what other experiments he was conducting, and uncover any further evidence of his treacherous manipulations. This laboratory was his stronghold, a secure facility guarded by cutting-edge technology and loyal military personnel – individuals who had probably already been subjected to Reed's various enhancements. This was a high-stakes gamble, a dangerous mission that could cost them everything.

Elara used her power to create diversions, masking their movements and manipulating the elements to provide cover for their infiltrations. Seraphina's telepathic abilities proved invaluable, allowing them to tap into the thoughts of their enemies, anticipating their every move. Marcus, despite his volatile nature, proved a surprisingly effective distraction, causing chaos and confusion as they maneuvered through the heavily guarded facility. Thomas, the hunted, had now become the hunter – hunting a far more dangerous prey than any he had encountered before.

The infiltration was fraught with peril. Laser grids, automated sentries, and heavily armed guards posed constant threats. They moved like shadows, their enhanced abilities allowing them to circumvent security measures that would have defeated ordinary human beings. But the sheer scale of Reed's operation was astounding. The laboratory was not merely a place of research; it was a sprawling complex, a hive of activity, where countless horrifying experiments were being conducted.

They found evidence of further attempts to replicate their abilities – a grim testament to Reed's unrelenting ambition. They also discovered evidence of a far more sinister project, one that suggested the development of a weapon far more devastating than any conventional arms – a weapon capable of unleashing unprecedented devastation. This chilling discovery served to reinforce the urgency and the severity of their mission.

The infiltration eventually brought them to Reed himself, a gaunt figure surrounded by the fruits of his terrifying ambition. He stood surrounded by screens displaying the progress of his latest project. He didn't show fear. Instead, a chilling, calculating smile spread across his face.

"You've come to join me," he stated calmly, eyes devoid of remorse, devoid of any human sentiment. "To contribute to the evolution of mankind."

His words were a twisted mockery of their shared past, a grotesque distortion of scientific progress, a testament to his obsession with control and dominance. The battle for the future of humanity had truly begun. The revolution had reached its climax, a final confrontation between a twisted genius and his augmented creations. The weight of the world and the legacy of Tempête rested on their shoulders. The fight for humanity's future was far from over.

The Serums Secret

The air in the catacombs hung heavy with the scent of damp earth and unspoken anxieties. Irina, her eyes glittering with a chilling intelligence, traced a finger along a crumbling wall, her expression unreadable. Elara, her face pale and drawn, nervously adjusted the worn leather satchel slung across her shoulder. Seraphina, her usually vibrant aura muted, sat hunched, her gaze fixed on the flickering candlelight. Thomas, the weight of his past and the burden of his mission pressing down on him felt a familiar chill crawling up his spine. He'd orchestrated this meeting, but the silence spoke volumes, a symphony of fear and uncertainty.

"The serum," Irina finally broke the silence, her voice a low, measured whisper that echoed in the confined space. "It's not just about erasing memories."

Elara looked up, startled. "What do you mean?"

Irina gestured towards the satchel. "I've been analyzing samples. Dr. Reed's notes hinted at something... more." She pulled out a small vial filled with a viscous, opalescent liquid. It shimmered with an inner light, almost ethereal in its beauty. "This isn't simply a memory eraser. It's a... re-writer."

A collective gasp escaped the three. Thomas felt a jolt, a sudden, visceral understanding of the implications. If the serum could rewrite memories, it could rewrite identities, personalities, even... destinies. The possibilities were terrifying.

"He could have used it on us," Seraphina whispered, her voice laced with horror. "To control us completely. To make us... obedient."

The thought hung in the air, heavy and suffocating. The brutal training, the relentless pursuit, the chilling obedience they'd exhibited – could it have been more than just conditioning? Could it have been the serum subtly altering its very essence?

"But why stop there?" Elara added, her voice trembling. "If he could rewrite memories, he could create entirely new identities, new individuals loyal only to him. An army. A perfect, unquestioning army."

Thomas felt a wave of nausea wash over him. He'd always known Reed was obsessed with control, but this was a level of manipulation he hadn't even considered. The implications were staggering. The serum wasn't just a tool for silencing the past; it was a weapon capable of forging the future, shaping the very fabric of reality.

Irina continued, her voice unwavering despite the chilling implications, "Reed's notes also mention unforeseen side effects – neurological degradation, personality fragmentation, catastrophic mental instability. The process is inherently unstable, prone to… unpredictable mutations."

The weight of that statement settled heavily on them. The serum wasn't a precise instrument; it was a gamble with the human psyche, a dangerous experiment with potentially devastating consequences. The thought of Reed unleashing this instability on a wider scale sent shivers down their spines. The possibility of a mass-produced army, riddled with mental instability and prone to unpredictable outbursts, was more terrifying than any superpowered foe.

"We need to find out more," Thomas said, his voice regaining its steely edge. The shock was giving way to a resolute determination. "We need to understand how this serum works, its limitations, its potential… its dangers."

The task before them was daunting. They were dealing with a weapon far more insidious than anything they'd faced before. But the alternative – allowing Reed to unleash this power on the world – was unthinkable.

Over the next few weeks, the four worked tirelessly. Irina used her exceptional intellect to decipher Reed's complex notes, painstakingly piecing together fragments of information. Elara, with her subtle manipulation of the elements, helped them create a secure, hidden laboratory within the catacombs, shielded from prying eyes and electronic surveillance. Seraphina, her telepathic abilities honed by years of survival, helped them identify and neutralize any potential threats. Thomas, haunted by his past but driven by his newfound purpose, provided the logistical support and tactical expertise they desperately needed.

Their research revealed a chilling picture. The serum wasn't just a simple chemical compound; it was a complex biological weapon, interacting with the brain's neural pathways in ways that were still largely unknown. It could selectively erase, rewrite, or even entirely reconstruct memories, leaving no trace of the original neural patterns. But the process was delicate, prone to errors, and the long-term effects were unpredictable and potentially catastrophic. The mutations Irina had alluded to were not mere speculation; they were a documented reality in Reed's notes, a grim testament to the serum's inherent instability. Some subjects had experienced complete personality collapses, while others developed bizarre and violent psychoses. A few even demonstrated spontaneous and unpredictable abilities—manifestations of latent human potential unleashed in uncontrolled and unpredictable ways.

As their understanding of the serum deepened, so did their fear. This wasn't just a weapon; it was a Pandora's Box, capable of unleashing chaos on an unimaginable scale. The possibilities for misuse were endless, from creating compliant soldiers and assassins to manipulating entire populations, erasing histories, rewriting narratives, and ultimately, controlling the very fabric of reality.

Their investigation also unearthed a sinister truth about Tempete's early experiments. The original goal of curing consumption had been a cover story. The true objective, hidden within layers of encrypted data and coded messages, was to explore the limits of human potential to push the boundaries of human biology to create the ultimate weapon. Tempête had not merely stumbled upon the ability to enhance human capabilities;

they had systematically and ruthlessly sought to exploit and control them.

The realization was a bitter pill to swallow. Their enhanced abilities, the very powers they had struggled to control and harness, were the product of a concealed project built on exploitation and manipulation. They had been pawns in a grand game, unwitting participants in a macabre experiment designed to serve the darkest ambitions of the military and, now, of Dr. Reed.

The weight of this new knowledge was crushing. Their fight was no longer merely a struggle for survival; it was a battle to prevent the annihilation of humanity itself. They were racing against time, against Reed's relentless pursuit of his twisted vision, a vision that threatened to erase history, redefine reality, and unleash chaos that could obliterate the world. The stakes were higher than ever before. The fight for humanity's future, a future that once seemed distant and uncertain, was now a desperate, immediate struggle against a foe wielding a power that could redefine the very concept of human existence. And the clock was ticking.

The Mutants Future

The flickering candlelight cast long, dancing shadows on the rough-hewn walls of the catacombs, illuminating the grim determination etched on the faces of the gathered mutants. The weight of their shared past, the brutal training, the relentless pursuit by Thomas – it all pressed down on them, a suffocating blanket of fear and uncertainty. Yet, amidst the oppressive atmosphere, a fragile spark of hope flickered. They were free, at least for now. But freedom, they were learning, came at a steep price.

Irina, her mind a whirlwind of calculations and strategies, spoke first, her voice a low hum that resonated with an unsettling clarity. "Reed's obsession… it's not merely scientific ambition. It's something… darker. He seeks to control, to reshape humanity in his own twisted image." She tapped a finger against a worn map spread out on the damp stone floor, a schematic of hidden tunnels and abandoned facilities, remnants of Tempete's covert operations. "He's accelerating his research. The memory serum… it's only the beginning."

Elara, her eyes reflecting the candlelight, shivered. The thought of Reed's unbridled power sent a chill down her spine. "He won't stop until he's created an army… an army of enhanced individuals, loyal only to him. An army that can rewrite history, erase dissent, and conquer the world." A tremor ran through her, a manifestation of her power, a subtle shift in the air pressure, hinting at the storm brewing within her. The very idea of such power in the hands of someone like Reed was terrifying. She imagined a world reshaped, its landscapes altered, its very climate weaponized against its own population, a horrifying vision fueled by her own ability to control the elements.

Seraphina, her telepathic senses straining, picked up the undercurrent of fear and anxiety rippling through the group. She closed her eyes, focusing on the task of calming their frayed nerves. "We need a plan," she whispered, her voice barely audible above the drip, drip, drip of water echoing through the subterranean tunnels. "We need to find a way to stop him before it's too late." Her telepathic scans revealed the chaotic thoughts of the others: fear, doubt, determination, a swirling vortex of emotions that reflected the gravity of their predicament.

Marcus, his pyrokinetic abilities simmering just beneath the surface, clenched his fists. The anger he felt was a palpable thing, a burning rage fueled by the injustices he had endured. "We fight," he growled, his voice thick with suppressed fury. "We fight for our lives, for the future, for a world where Reed's abominations cannot thrive." The flames within him, though contained, threatened to erupt, a testament to the volatile mix of power and resentment that coursed through his veins. The sheer destructive power he possessed terrified him, even as it fueled his resolve.

Thomas, burdened by the weight of his past actions, remained silent for a long moment, the memories of his relentless pursuit of his former colleagues a heavy burden. He'd been a weapon, a tool, and the guilt gnawed at him. The weight of his past, the blood on his hands, threatened to drown him. He had been a puppet, manipulated by Reed, and the thought that he had been used to hunt his own kin was a wound that would never fully heal. He looked at his former comrades, their faces etched with worry and determination, and felt a wave of shame. But he couldn't dwell on the past; they needed him. His unique skills – his enhanced senses, his heightened reflexes – were their best chance of survival. He needed to atone for his past, to use his abilities to protect those he had once hunted.

"We need to understand Reed's plan," Thomas finally said, his voice low and measured. "We need to find out what he's working on next, what other enhancements he's pursuing." His analytical mind, honed through years of brutal training, began to piece together the puzzle. "The memory serum… it's a means to an end. It's a way to erase witnesses, to control the narrative." He paused, his gaze sweeping over their faces, each one bearing the scars of their past. "We were all products of his ambition, tools to be used and discarded. But we're no longer just pawns in his game. We are the resistance."

Irina added, "We need to leverage our individual strengths. Elara, your control over the weather could provide diversions and create chaos. Seraphina, your telepathy can be used for reconnaissance to anticipate Reed's moves. Marcus, your pyrokinesis... use it sparingly but strategically." She turned to Thomas. "And you, Thomas, your enhanced senses and reflexes will be invaluable in infiltration and close-quarters combat. We cannot afford to fail."

Days turned into weeks as the mutants worked tirelessly, meticulously planning their next move. They used hidden tunnels and abandoned subway lines to navigate the city, avoiding detection. Seraphina's telepathic abilities proved crucial, allowing them to anticipate Reed's movements and avoid his patrols. Elara's control over the weather provided effective cover, masking their movements and creating diversions. Marcus's pyrokinesis was a terrifying weapon used cautiously but effectively to disable obstacles and neutralize threats. Thomas, with his heightened senses, served as their eyes and ears, guiding them through the treacherous urban landscape.

Their investigation led them to a secluded laboratory hidden deep beneath the city, a forgotten remnant of Tempete's operations. It was here that Reed was conducting his most recent experiments. They discovered his work wasn't just limited to the memory serum. He had developed a new serum – more potent, more dangerous – one that could amplify the abilities of existing mutants, transforming them into something far beyond their initial capabilities. The implications were terrifying. Reed wasn't just creating new mutants; he was escalating the power of those he already had under his control, creating an unstoppable army.

The mutants faced a difficult choice. They could try to destroy the laboratory, but that might alert Reed and his army. They could also try to steal the serum, hoping to weaponize it against him. But if it fell into the wrong hands, the consequences could be catastrophic. Irina's tactical brilliance and Seraphina's keen insights helped them devise a daring plan, one that balanced the need for immediate action with the necessity of long-term strategy. They would infiltrate the laboratory, gather information, and leave a trail of carefully placed disruptions that would delay Reed's progress without causing a full-scale alarm.

Their mission was fraught with peril. They faced heavily armed guards, sophisticated security systems, and Reed's own enhanced individuals – loyal soldiers who the new serum had further augmented. The battle was intense, a terrifying dance between super-powered individuals. Thomas, shedding the vestiges of his past, fought with a ferocity that surprised even himself, his enhanced senses guiding him through the chaos. Elara unleashed a storm of rain and wind, creating diversions and hindering Reed's forces. Marcus's pyrokinesis blazed through the corridors, a fiery torrent that consumed enemies and disabled security systems. Seraphina, her mind a battlefield in itself, used her telepathy to disrupt the enemy's coordination and sow discord among their ranks. Irina, orchestrating their every move, ensured their survival.

In the end, they succeeded in gathering crucial information about Reed's work and disrupting his plans. The mission was harrowing, but the mutants emerged victorious, battered but not broken. They had proven that even against overwhelming odds, their combined strength could prevail. They emerged from the ruins of the laboratory, their faces grim but their spirits undeterred. The fight had just begun. They knew that Reed would not give up easily. His obsession, his thirst for power, was too great. But they also knew they would not give up either. They had tasted freedom, and they would fight to the very end to preserve it. The future of humanity rested on their shoulders, a future now shaped by a terrifying new reality of super-powered individuals and unchecked scientific ambition. The fight for survival continued, a desperate race against time against power that could rewrite the very fabric of reality.

Chapter 9: Aftermath

The Military's Response

The earth trembled, not with seismic fury, but with the controlled explosions of a methodically planned military response. The escape of the Tempête mutants wasn't just a breach of security; it was a catastrophic failure of the regime's most ambitious – and terrifying – project. General Petrov, the man who had overseen the weaponization of the enhanced individuals, felt the full weight of that failure crushing him. His carefully constructed world, a world where super-powered soldiers would guarantee the nation's dominance, lay in ruins.

The immediate response was brutal and swift. Every avenue of escape was sealed off. Major cities went on high alert, the streets patrolled by heavily armed soldiers, their faces grim under the harsh glare of searchlights. The air crackled with the tension of a nation on the brink. The escape of Irina, Elara, Seraphina, and Marcus wasn't simply a desertion; it was an act of rebellion against the military's power. The media, strictly controlled in those days, reported only a vague story of a prison break, omitting any mention of enhanced abilities. The public remained unaware of the true nature of the escaped prisoners.

However, the higher ranks of the military were in a state of panic. Petrov's superiors demanded answers, answers he didn't have. The meticulously crafted plans for using the mutants as weapons had been torn to shreds by Irina's calculated escape. He ordered a full-scale manhunt, deploying specialist units trained in unconventional warfare. He knew tracking enhanced individuals would require more than brute force. They needed someone who understood their capabilities, someone who knew their weaknesses – and that person, tragically, was Thomas.

The irony wasn't lost on Petrov. Thomas, the perfect soldier, the ultimate weapon, had failed. Or had he? Petrov entertained a horrifying possibility: Thomas's betrayal wasn't a sudden act of defiance. It was a calculated maneuver, a meticulously planned infiltration into the enemy camp. He imagined Thomas feeding information to the mutants, guiding them, protecting them. The thought was chilling; the idea of one of his own weapons turned against him. This was a far more dangerous proposition than the initial escape.

The manhunt became a race against time, a desperate attempt to recapture the lost assets before they could wreak havoc or, worse, expose the truth behind Tempête. The military's response wasn't solely focused on capturing the mutants. It was equally concerned with erasing the project's existence, destroying all evidence of Tempete's existence before the public could find out. This required a level of secrecy unprecedented, even in those times of political intrigue.

The fallout within the military was immense. Careers were ruined, and reputations destroyed. Petrov, despite his desperation, clung to his position, desperately trying to reclaim control amidst the chaos. He knew that the exposure of Tempête would not only shatter the military's reputation but could also trigger international incidents and destabilize the fragile peace that prevailed in Europe. The repercussions could be devastating and would result in political upheaval to economic ruin.

The scientists involved, those who hadn't erased their memories, were also subject to intense scrutiny. Dr. Reed, the unwavering believer in the project's potential, became a particular target of investigation. His loyalty, always questioned, was now actively doubted. He was a loose end, a potential whistleblower who could unleash a storm of controversy. He knew the depth of the project's secrecy and its potential damage if exposed.

The hunt for the escaped mutants turned into a desperate attempt to control the narrative. A battle fought not just on the streets but also in the shadowy corridors of power. The military's propaganda machine went into overdrive, spreading carefully crafted disinformation to deflect any public attention from the true nature of the escaped individuals.

Meanwhile, Thomas's betrayal sent shockwaves throughout the military hierarchy. He was more than just a soldier; he was a testament to the project's success. His defection represented a profound moral failure, a crack in the seemingly impenetrable wall of discipline and obedience. The military's rigid structure had been violated; its authority was challenged by one of its own. The implications were far-reaching. Trust, already tenuous, was shattered amongst the ranks. Suspicion reigned supreme. Paranoia became a contagious disease, infecting every level of the command structure. The whispers and rumors of potential traitors created an atmosphere of distrust and fear.

The aftermath wasn't only limited to the military. The scientific community was rocked by the revelations surrounding Tempête. The ethical implications of creating super-powered individuals and the moral questions surrounding the manipulation of human life for military purposes – were issues that would haunt the world for decades to come. The project had cast a long shadow, raising questions about the boundaries of scientific advancement and the responsibility of scientists to their creations. The public, largely kept in the dark about the Tempête project, only sensed the growing unease reflected in the heightened military presence and the tightened restrictions on information. The unspoken fear that something monstrous lay hidden beneath the surface created a sense of collective unease.

The hunt continued, but it was now a different kind of hunt. It wasn't simply about recapturing escaped prisoners; it was about containing a catastrophic breach of national security, silencing potential whistleblowers, and maintaining the illusion of control in a world where their most potent weapon had turned against them. The military's response was a testament to the lengths they were willing to go to suppress the truth, a testament to the lengths of their fear. The true cost of Tempête was far from settled, the ripples of its catastrophic fallout extending far beyond the immediate aftermath of the escape into a future riddled with uncertainty and shadowed by the enduring legacy of fear.

The Fallout Of Tempête

The dust settled, literally and figuratively. The scorched earth of the escape route, a testament to the military's brutal attempts to recapture the Tempête mutants, lay silent under a bruised, twilight sky. The air, thick with the sharp smell of burnt vegetation and ozone, held a lingering tension, a palpable sense of what had been lost and what remained at stake. General Petrov, his face etched with a weariness that opposed years of ruthless ambition, stared out at the devastation. The meticulously planned operation, designed to swiftly and silently neutralize the threat, had devolved into a chaotic, destructive mess. The escape, while stunning in its audacity, had exposed the horrifying truth behind Tempête – a truth that threatened to unravel the very fabric of national security.

The immediate aftermath saw a flurry of activity. It was a desperate attempt to control the narrative. Censorship tightened its iron grip; news reports spoke of a tragic accident, a rogue military exercise gone awry. The public, largely unaware of the existence of the Tempête mutants, was fed a carefully crafted lie. Yet, the whispers began to spread, carried on the wind, in hushed conversations in smoky backrooms, and in the anxious glances exchanged across crowded streets. The truth, like a persistent weed, stubbornly refused to be silenced.

The long-term repercussions, however, proved far more insidious than the immediate fallout. The military's cover-up, while initially effective, began to unravel at its seams. The sheer scale of the operation, the resources deployed, the level of destruction – these were not easily explained away. Whispers turned into rumors, rumors into speculation, and speculation into a simmering public distrust of the government. This erosion of trust reached far beyond the simple matter of the escaped mutants. It chipped away at the very foundations of authority, casting a long shadow over the nation's political landscape.

The scientists involved, or rather, the surviving scientists lived under a shroud of fear. Dr. Reed, the unwavering believer, continued his work, fueled by a twisted sense of scientific purpose. He secretly sought ways to improve the process, to create even more powerful soldiers, oblivious to the moral abyss that had already engulfed his project. His colleagues, however, haunted by their creation, suffered in silence. The memory-erasing serum, while offering a temporary reprieve from the horrors they had witnessed, left gaping holes in their lives, fragmented memories and a lingering sense of incompleteness, a constant reminder of their past sins.

The mutants themselves, scattered across the globe, faced a different kind of fallout. Elara, with her power over the weather, became a recluse, her fear of being discovered outweighing her own internal turmoil. Irina, with her unparalleled intellect, struggled with the loneliness that came with exceptional abilities, constantly looking over her shoulder, her extraordinary mind unable to provide solace from the constant threat of capture. Dmitri, raw strength concealed under a veneer of quiet contemplation, found his existence a constant battle against the urges that gnawed within. Seraphina, blessed with telepathy, bore the additional burden of other people's fears, her mind a frenzy of anxieties and desperation. Marcus, consumed by his pyrokinesis, wrestled with the flames both within and without. Only Thomas remained in service, a silent executioner, his sense of purpose utterly devoid of humanity.

The economic consequences were equally devastating. The vast resources poured into Tempête, the lost productivity from the widespread disruption caused by the escape, and the ongoing cost of the extensive military search and surveillance placed an unbearable strain on the nation's economy. The public outcry against the mismanagement of funds grew, fueling anti-government sentiment and pushing the country towards a deep and prolonged economic crisis.

The social fallout was perhaps the most profound. The very fabric of society began to fray. The lines between reality and fiction blurred; the nation's collective consciousness was fractured, unable to reconcile the official narrative with the growing sense of unease. Fear of the unknown gnawed at the hearts of the populace; suspicion replaced trust, and paranoia became the new normal. The project's secrecy and its eventual exposure undermined the public's faith not only in the government but also in science itself.

The impact on the military was immense. General Petrov, stripped of his command and his reputation tarnished, faced a future shrouded in uncertainty. The military's credibility was shattered. Public trust, already eroded, dwindled even further. The event sparked a wide-ranging debate within the armed forces about the ethics of scientific advancements and the potential dangers of unchecked military ambition. The incident served as a potent reminder of the immense responsibility that accompanied power. The organization became consumed by infighting and investigations, and its once-impeccable efficiency was severely hampered.

Years later, the scars of Tempête remained. The economic downturn lasted for decades, leaving a legacy of poverty and social unrest. The memory of the incident served as a stark warning, a ghost that haunted the collective consciousness. Rumors of the mutants persisted, fueling legends and myths, their stories becoming increasingly embellished, their identities blurred into folklore. The true cost of Tempête went far beyond the immediate casualties and the destruction. The long-term effects were profound, impacting every facet of the nation, a grim testament to the perilous nature of unchecked ambition and the ethical dilemmas that came with scientific progress. The project's legacy served as a cautionary tale, a reminder of the potential for scientific advancements to be twisted for nefarious purposes and the devastating consequences that followed. The world changed irrevocably, marked forever by the fallout of Tempête – a reminder that progress, unchecked, could lead to ruin and that even the most ambitious of projects could leave behind a legacy of fear, mistrust and despair. The shadow of Tempête, long after the echoes of the explosions had faded, continued to loom large, a constant reminder of the dangerous path paved by unchecked scientific ambition and the horrifying consequences that ensued.

The world learned a harsh lesson from Tempête – a lesson about the limits of control, the dangers of ambition, and the enduring power of truth. The whispers persisted, a subterranean current flowing beneath the surface of carefully constructed narratives, a testament to the enduring human capacity for remembering even when official stories try to bury the truth. The cost of Tempête was far from settled. Its consequences continued to ripple through time, a grim reminder that the true measure of scientific progress lay not just in its advancements but in its ethical implications and its ultimate cost to humanity.

The Scientists Fate

The silence in the abandoned laboratory was heavier than the dust motes dancing in the slivers of sunlight piercing the grimy windows. Dr. Dubois, his usually meticulous lab coat stained and torn, stared at the empty vials, the ghostly remnants of the memory-erasing serum. The air hung thick with the unspoken, the weight of their collective guilt a palpable entity in the room. He ran a trembling hand over his scalp, a phantom ache lingering where his memories used to reside. The serum had worked too well, perhaps. The sharp edges of their culpability, the horrifying clarity of their actions, were blunted, softened, yet a nagging unease, a persistent shadow, remained.

Dr. Moreau, her face drawn and pale, sat hunched over a discarded notebook, its pages filled with frantic scribbles, a testament to the frantic race to erase their past. The meticulous calculations, the intricate formulas, now served only as a morbid reminder of their hubris. She picked up a photograph – a faded image of a younger, more hopeful her, standing beside Dr. Reed, their faces alight with the optimism that had fueled their early experiments. Now, that optimism felt like a cruel betrayal, a phantom limb of a life that no longer existed. The image slipped from her numb fingers, the crackle of the ageing paper mirroring the fracturing of her own shattered psyche.

Dr. Petrova, ever the pragmatist, was less focused on the emotional fallout and more concerned with the practical implications of their actions. She meticulously organized the remaining research materials, her movements precise, almost robotic, a stark contrast to the turmoil raging within her. The serum, while successful in erasing their memories of Tempête, had left a void, a gaping chasm in their consciousness, a space where their past should have been. The memories may have vanished, but the lingering guilt, the unspoken knowledge of their transgressions, remained a constant, insidious companion. The silence was broken only by the rhythmic scratch of her pen as she carefully cataloged their research, a grim undertaking that felt both necessary and futile. She knew that the world had moved on, unaware of the monstrous secret they had buried, but the weight of it pressed down on them, an invisible burden that could not be erased, no matter how effective the serum proved to be.

Dr. Thorne, the youngest of the group, was the most visibly affected. His youthful idealism, once so vibrant, was now a flickering candle in the gale of his remorse. He wandered the lab, his gaze flitting from one object to another as if searching for a tangible link to his lost memories, to the past that had been surgically removed from his mind. The serum had left him adrift, a ghost in his own life, unable to fully grasp the person he was or the horrors he had participated in. His hands shook as he touched a chipped test tube, the cold glass a stark reminder of the cold, calculated cruelty that had driven their work. The weight of his past, even veiled in the mists of amnesia, felt like a physical burden, constricting his chest, suffocating him with silent despair. He couldn't articulate the source of his anxiety; he only knew that something terrible had happened, something that left a gaping wound in his soul.

The silence in the laboratory was broken only by the occasional sigh, the rustle of papers, and the sporadic clatter of a dropped vial. The atmosphere was heavy with unspoken regrets, the ghost of what had been. The serum had erased their memories, but it hadn't erased their guilt. It hadn't erased the ethical dilemma they had created, the monstrous implications of their scientific endeavors. The weight of their actions, the potential consequences of their work, hung over them like a shroud, a constant, inescapable reminder of the cost of unchecked ambition and the fragility of human morality. The eradication of their memories had not provided solace; it had created a vacuum of unknown horror.

Their escape was not a successful flight to freedom but a desperate flight from the consequences of their actions. They had fled not just the military but also the spectre of their own past, the monstrous legacy of Tempête. Yet, the shadow of their creation followed them, clinging to them like a second skin, a constant reminder of their role in unleashing chaos onto the world. They had sought refuge in oblivion but found only a different kind of torment: a persistent, nameless dread that gnawed at the edges of their consciousness, a testament to the enduring power of guilt, even when memory itself is erased.

The decision to erase their memories had been a desperate act of self-preservation, a misguided attempt to atone for their sins by obliterating their awareness of them. But the human psyche is not so easily manipulated. The subconscious, a relentless, probing entity, held onto fragments of their past, fragments that manifested as anxiety, as nightmares, as the persistent, unshakeable feeling that something terrible had transpired. The absence of explicit memories only heightened the mystery, fueling their internal torment. The erased details haunted them in fragmented shadows and unsettling half-dreams.

They had traded conscious guilt for a nameless dread, a constant state of unease that permeated every aspect of their lives. They were shadows of their former selves, adrift in a sea of forgotten memories yet burdened by an inescapable sense of loss and guilt. Their escape was not a victory; it was a retreat into a twilight zone of amnesia, where they remained prisoners of their own consciences, even in the absence of conscious memory.

Dr. Reed remained. His unwavering belief in the potential of their work, in the ultimate benefit that could be derived from their enhancements, stood in stark contrast to the despair of his colleagues. He, alone, possessed the complete picture, the full understanding of the project's complexities and its inherent risks. He had not taken the serum, choosing instead to bear the burden of their collective guilt, the chilling knowledge of their creation. His decision was driven by a complex mix of unwavering faith in science, a terrifying sense of responsibility, and, perhaps, a touch of hubris. He believed that the potential benefits of their work outweighed the ethical concerns and that the progress they had made, however terrifying, was ultimately worth it. His colleagues, however, disagreed, their experiences shaping them into cautious, frightened shadows of their former scientific selves.

Reed's faith was a lonely beacon in the encroaching darkness. He was the lone keeper of their secrets, the sole inheritor of their legacy. The future, however, remained uncertain. The implications of Tempête were far-reaching and deeply unsettling. The weaponization of genetic enhancement, the potential for widespread misuse, the unpredictable nature of the mutants – these were all issues that haunted him, too. But unlike his colleagues, he was not paralyzed by fear and remorse. He saw a future where their work could be harnessed for good, a future where the power they had unleashed could be controlled and used to benefit humanity. He had chosen a different path, one fraught with risk and uncertainty, a path defined by both unwavering ambition and a deep, disturbing awareness of his own moral ambiguity.

The fate of the scientists was not simply a matter of physical survival or escape. It was a profound exploration of the ethical implications of scientific advancement, a chilling testament to the human capacity for both extraordinary achievement and devastating failure. They had sought to cure disease, but instead, they had created monsters, and in doing so, they had created monsters within themselves. The memory-erasing serum had offered a temporary reprieve, a false sense of peace. Still, the underlying issues of their guilt, their role in the unleashing of a terrifying power, remained deeply ingrained in their very beings. Their lives after Tempête were not a happy ending but a complex, emotionally echoing continuation of their story, a stark reminder that the pursuit of knowledge, without a parallel consideration for its ethical implications, can have devastating consequences. The cost of their scientific ambition was far from settled. It had become a stubborn part of their identities, a haunting testament to the dark side of human progress.

Thomas's Redemption

The mountain air bit at Thomas's exposed skin, a stark contrast to the stifling, sterile environment of the military labs he'd known for so long. He hadn't felt the biting chill of true winter in years, a testament to the controlled climates of his imprisonment and the following years spent hunting his former comrades. He'd hunted them with a chilling efficiency, a precision honed by relentless training and an unshakeable obedience instilled through fear and pain. But the faces of Irina, Elara, Seraphina, and even the volatile Marcus, haunted his dreams, the vibrant colors of their escape stark against the monochrome palette of his existence.

He'd been a tool, a weapon. Now, standing on the precipice of a snow-covered peak, watching the sun bleed across the horizon, he felt the weight of that realization crush him. The serum, the memory-erasing serum that Tempête had developed, had not touched him. His memories, though fragmented and clouded at the edges by the years of intense conditioning, were still his. He remembered the horrors, the experiments, the brutal training, but he also remembered Irina's quick wit and Elara's quiet strength. They were not just targets; they were people.

He'd been ordered to eliminate them, to silence them permanently, yet their survival, their defiance, chipped away at the foundation of his programming. He'd witnessed their struggle, their desperation, their courage in the face of his relentless pursuit. He had seen the fear in their eyes, the very fear that his own actions had generated. The fear, however, had not been for their own lives alone but for what they had unknowingly unleashed upon the world. Their fear reflected his growing understanding of their predicament and his own profound moral conflict. For years he had fulfilled his role as a hunter; he had become the beast he had been created to be. He had been successful, but at what cost?

The weight of this realization pressed upon him heavily. He found himself drawn to the remote mountain regions, seeking solitude not in the form of isolation but in a kind of quiet contemplation. The harsh beauty of the wilderness mirrored the turmoil within him. He began to understand that his redemption would not be found in simply abandoning his mission; it would require a far more profound transformation. He needed to confront his past, not just the actions he had taken but the beliefs that had driven him.

He started small. He rescued a lost hiker, a lone figure struggling against the unforgiving landscape, much like his former comrades had struggled against his own unforgiving actions. The act was simple, almost instinctual, yet the ripple effect surprised him. The gratitude in the hiker's eyes, the sense of connection, even if fleeting, was a stark contrast to the blank, fearful stares he'd become accustomed to. He began leaving anonymous donations to local charities, his enhanced senses helping him locate those in genuine need, unnoticed by others but meticulously targeted by him.

The silence was no longer oppressive but rather a space for reflection. He spent countless nights under the vast, indifferent sky, wrestling with his past. He was not trying to erase his past, nor to forget his actions, but rather to understand them, to integrate them into a new narrative, one where he was not just a hunter but a man capable of compassion and amends.

His enhanced senses, once used as tools of pursuit, now served as instruments of help. He could hear the silent cries for help hidden in the cacophony of city noises, the subtle shifts in air pressure that signaled danger, often far beyond the capabilities of normal human senses. He used these to help discreetly and anonymously, never revealing his true identity or his past.

He found solace in helping others, not as a means of self-forgiveness, but as a way to gradually reorient his existence and build a sense of self beyond the constraints of his programming. Each act of kindness, each selfless deed, became a small step towards a different kind of self, a redemption built not on denial or avoidance but on active participation in the rebuilding of a world that his past had helped to unravel. He moved towards a more humane trajectory, away from the path of death and destruction that he had known for so long.

The process was excruciatingly slow, a torturous climb out of the abyss of his past. Doubt gnawed at him constantly. Could he ever truly atone for his actions? Could he ever fully escape the shadow of the man he'd been? He often found himself questioning the efficacy of his actions and the meaning of his existence. He still felt the phantom ache of orders given, the phantom weight of responsibilities that no longer existed. He was still Thomas, the enhanced being created by Tempête, but he was also becoming something else, something more.

He started to read, devouring books on philosophy, ethics, and history. He sought to understand the human condition, the complexities of morality, the nuances of right and wrong, all to place his own experiences within a broader context, to make sense of the choices he had made, and the path he was now forging for himself. He sought understanding not in the realm of science but in the depths of the human spirit, seeking the answer not in the laboratory but within his own soul.

One day, he stumbled across a news report about a group working to rehabilitate former child soldiers. It was then that he saw his path. He would use his skills, his unique abilities, to help those who, like him, had been victims of manipulation, victims of systems that used individuals for their own nefarious purposes. His enhanced senses would become a tool not of destruction but of protection, a shield against further exploitation and pain.

He started volunteering, initially anonymously, his abilities, making his contributions invaluable. He identified children in need, provided them with safe passage out of danger, and often used his enhanced healing abilities to treat their physical and emotional wounds. His work involved a great deal of risk, but Thomas had come to find that his sense of purpose was not found in hiding nor in avoidance of consequences but rather in his ability to help others.

He found satisfaction in the small acts of kindness that brought comfort and hope to these fragile souls. This satisfaction exceeded any fleeting thrill he'd experienced during his time as an assassin. The redemption was not a sudden epiphany, a grand gesture that washed away years of guilt, but rather a slow, painstaking process of rebuilding, a testament to the resilience of the human spirit and a profound illustration of the transformative power of self-reflection and atonement.

His path to redemption was not easy, but in the quiet moments, in the acts of service, and in the healing touch extended to those in need, Thomas found a measure of peace. The ghosts of his past still lingered, a somber reminder of his actions, but they no longer held the same power, the same paralyzing hold over his existence. He was no longer defined by the horrors he'd committed; he was slowly building a new identity, one forged in the crucible of his past but shaped by a commitment to a better future. The cost of his redemption would be a lifelong journey of service and atonement, but it was a journey he willingly embraced, a path towards a future where his past could be understood as a part of him, not as a definition of him. The quiet acceptance that he could never fully erase his past was crucial to his continuing journey. He had found a way to live with it, to use it as fuel for a life dedicated to healing both himself and others. He had found his redemption not in forgetting but in remembering and using the memory to make amends. The echoes of Tempête, once symbols of fear and horror, were now transformed into a catalyst for a new kind of life, a new kind of humanity.

The Legacy Of Tempête

The whispers about Tempête, initially confined to hushed conversations in the shadowy corners of intelligence agencies and secret research facilities, began to bleed into the public consciousness. It started subtly – a strange cluster of unexplained weather events, a series of seemingly impossible accidents involving individuals displaying superhuman abilities. Newspapers, initially dismissing the rumors as sensationalism, found themselves grappling with a growing body of evidence that suggested something extraordinary had occurred. The unexplained disappearances of several prominent scientists, and the whispers of a secret organization codenamed Tempête all fueled the flames of speculation.

The official response was, predictably, denial. Governments, implicated either directly or indirectly in the Tempête project, worked tirelessly to suppress information, distributing carefully crafted narratives that dismissed any connection between the unusual events and any government-sponsored research. Yet, the cracks in the façade of official secrecy widened with each passing year. Leaked documents, anonymous testimonies, and the occasional inexplicable display of superhuman capabilities in public served as constant reminders of the project's existence.

The impact on the scientific community was profound. The ethical implications of Tempête cast a long shadow over scientific research, creating a climate of suspicion and mistrust. Funding for ambitious projects dwindled as governments and private institutions alike grew hesitant to invest in research that could potentially yield unpredictable and dangerous results. The once-unbridled enthusiasm for scientific advancement was replaced by a cautious approach, burdened by the fear of repeating Tempete's mistakes. The era of unchecked ambition, characteristic of the pre-Tempête years, was over.

The lingering effects on society were equally significant. The very nature of reality had been subtly altered, forever touched by the specter of superhuman abilities. The potential for chaos, manipulation, and the abuse of power became a constant source of anxiety. Governments implemented stricter security measures fueled by a deep-seated fear of individuals who could potentially defy the limitations of ordinary human capacity. Paranoia and suspicion became commonplace, eroding public trust in authority. The sense of vulnerability, a shared anxiety over the potential misuse of scientific power, became a defining characteristic of the era.

The legacy of Tempête extended far beyond the immediate fallout of the project. It fundamentally reshaped the landscape of international relations. The knowledge that such powerful individuals existed and the potential for their weaponization dramatically altered the geopolitical landscape. Nations engaged in a clandestine arms race, striving to develop countermeasures and strategies to control or exploit the potential of enhanced individuals. The line between conventional warfare and unconventional conflict became increasingly blurred, leading to a new era of strategic uncertainty.

Economically, the impact of Tempête was complex and far-reaching. The initial disruption caused by the escape of the enhanced individuals and the subsequent attempts to recapture them led to widespread economic instability. However, the long-term implications were even more significant. The technology developed by Tempête, initially intended to create enhanced individuals, found its way into various other fields, yielding unforeseen benefits and consequences. Advancements in genetic engineering, biotechnology, and other scientific fields were accelerated, albeit with an increased emphasis on ethical considerations and stringent regulations. The economic boom that followed was shadowed by an undercurrent of fear, a constant reminder of the unpredictable nature of scientific progress.

In the decades following the disintegration of Tempête, the world witnessed the rise of a new type of underground culture. Individuals with minor enhancements, unintended byproducts of Tempete's research or subsequent experiments emerged from the shadows. These individuals formed their own communities, operating outside the reach of official scrutiny. Some embraced their abilities, using them for personal gain or to fight for what they believed in. Others lived in fear, hiding their capabilities to avoid persecution. This subculture posed a unique challenge to governments and intelligence agencies, forcing them to rethink their strategies for monitoring and controlling individuals with enhanced abilities. It also spurred a renewed debate on the ethical implications of scientific advancement and the inherent risks of tampering with the very fabric of human nature.

Thomas, though finding his own measure of peace, served as a living reminder of Tempete's legacy. His story, once whispered among the few who knew the truth, became a cautionary tale. He was a symbol of the potential for redemption but also of the indelible mark left by the project. His journey was a testament to the enduring power of the human spirit, a capacity for self-reflection and atonement, even after committing acts of unspeakable violence. But he also served as a stark reminder of the long shadow cast by unchecked scientific ambition and the moral dilemmas inherent in the pursuit of scientific breakthroughs.

The memory-erasing serum, a cruel byproduct of Tempete's relentless pursuit of power, remained a troubling enigma. Its existence raised questions about the moral boundaries of scientific intervention, the right to alter memories, and the very nature of identity. Its effects, though initially intended to provide oblivion, became a symbol of the lasting, often unseen consequences of reckless scientific ambition. The serum, a silent testament to the ethical complexities of scientific progress, served as a grim reminder of the dangers of unchecked scientific power. It served as a grim symbol of the potential for self-destruction inherent in the pursuit of scientific mastery, a stark warning against the temptation to wield scientific progress as a tool for achieving impossible goals.

The legacy of Tempête continued to shape the world, influencing everything from scientific policy to societal structures. The ethical debates sparked by the project lingered, ensuring that the moral complexities of scientific advancement remained at the forefront of public discourse. Tempête was not simply a scientific project; it was a cautionary tale, a stark reminder of the potential for scientific ambition to spiral out of control, leaving a trail of destruction in its wake. The whispers of Tempête served as a constant reminder, a ghostly echo reverberating throughout the decades, shaping the future in ways both visible and unseen. The world continued to grapple with the consequences of Tempête, a stark reminder that even the most well-intentioned scientific endeavors can have unforeseen and devastating consequences, reminding us that true progress lies not just in scientific achievement but in the ethical consideration that should govern its use. The memory of Tempête would forever be etched into the very fabric of human history, a testament to the profound impact scientific ambition can have on the world and a sobering reminder that the pursuit of knowledge must always be tempered with wisdom and a deep sense of responsibility.

Chapter 10: Echoes Of The Past

The New Generation

The Parisian rain, a relentless curtain of grey, mirrored the somber mood settling over the city. Five years had passed since the escape from the clandestine Tempête facility, five years since Thomas, the obedient weapon, had hunted his fellow mutants across the ravaged landscapes of Europe. Yet, the echoes of Tempete's disastrous legacy reverberated, not in the whispers of survivors, but in the burgeoning manifestations of a new generation.

A young woman, barely out of her teens, named Anya found herself plagued by inexplicable visions – fleeting glimpses of a world ablaze, of figures with impossible powers locked in a desperate struggle. These weren't ordinary hallucinations; they were fragments of memories, not her own, but echoes of a past she couldn't understand. Anya lived a quiet life in a small village nestled in the French countryside, far removed from the urban chaos and the whispers of the war's end. But the visions intensified, growing more vivid, more insistent, revealing snippets of a hidden world, a world of enhanced abilities and relentless pursuit. She discovered she possessed incredible speed, a blur of motion that left ordinary people gaping in disbelief. Her reflexes were sharper than any athlete's, her strength surpassing that of any man. These abilities, however, came at a cost; crippling migraines and moments of disorientation, a testament to her body's struggle to accommodate its newfound powers.

Meanwhile, in the sprawling industrial heart of Berlin, a young man named Kaspar displayed an uncanny control over electricity. He could manipulate currents with a thought, short-circuiting machines with a mere gesture. His life, however, was one of constant fear and suspicion. His power, unpredictable and often uncontrolled, resulted in accidents that left him ostracized. He lived on the fringes of society, a shadowy figure haunted by the possibility of discovery. Unlike Anya, Kaspar's memories remained intact, yet a deep-seated unease gnawed at him, a premonition of a dangerous destiny he couldn't quite grasp. He yearned for answers, searching desperately for some explanation for his unnerving abilities. He found solace only in the quiet hum of the electrical grid, feeling a strange connection to the unseen energy coursing beneath the city's streets.

These were not isolated incidents. Across Europe, whispers circulated, hushed conversations about individuals possessing extraordinary capabilities – individuals who appeared seemingly out of nowhere. These were the children of Tempête, the unintended legacy of the scientists' reckless ambition. The memory-erasing serum, designed to erase the guilt of the original Tempête scientists, had failed to anticipate the genetic imprint left on their subjects. It had proven to be only a temporary solution, its effects warning over time, leaving a new generation to inherit the burden of enhanced abilities and the threat of discovery.

Irina, having evaded Thomas's pursuit for years, had remained hidden in the shadow of the war's devastation. She'd spent the time building a network, a silent brotherhood of individuals with similar abilities, protecting them from the prying eyes of the authorities. Anya and Kaspar, along with others, found refuge within this network, learning to control their powers and understand their shared history. Irina knew their existence was a direct threat to the delicate peace that had finally settled upon the war-torn continent. The revelation that Tempete's work had not ended but merely evolved into a new, even more unpredictable threat was a truth both terrifying and empowering.

The ethical debate, dormant for a few years after the apparent demise of Tempête, re-emerged with renewed intensity. Scientists, once captivated by the potential of genetic manipulation, now grappled with the ethical implications of their work. The creation of these individuals had brought about unintended consequences, creating a generation burdened by powers they never asked for and a future shrouded in uncertainty. The world had been irrevocably altered by Tempete's experiments, forever questioning the boundaries of human potential and the cost of unchecked ambition.

Thomas, wrestling with the moral complexities of his past, found himself at a crossroads. He'd betrayed the military, choosing to protect his former colleagues, but the weight of his actions hung heavily upon him. He had spent years hunting down his friends, only to become a protector. The conflict between his ingrained obedience and his newly found empathy formed a constant internal struggle. The path towards redemption would be fraught with danger and self-doubt. His enhanced senses continued to alert him to a sense of impending doom.

The future remained uncertain, the shadows of Tempete's legacy stretching far into the unknown. Irina, haunted by the potential for further abuse of power, issued a stark warning – a cautionary tale of scientific hubris and the unpredictable consequences of tampering with the fundamental building blocks of life. The once-secret program had inadvertently seeded the world with individuals possessing extraordinary abilities. Still, only time would tell whether this new generation would become a force for good or a catalyst for further chaos. The world, forever altered by the echoes of Tempete's past, found itself on the precipice of a new era. In this era, the lines between man and mutant blurred, leaving the future as uncertain as the storm clouds gathering on the horizon.

The world, once scarred by the devastation of war, now faced a new and equally potent threat. The advancements in genetics that were once viewed as a beacon of hope had become a Pandora's Box, releasing a wave of enhanced individuals, a testament to the dangers of unchecked ambition. The clandestine world of Tempête, once buried beneath the sands of time, now resurfaced, threatening to destabilize the fragile peace that had finally been achieved. This new generation, inheriting the burden of powers they never asked for, found themselves facing a world that was ill-prepared for their existence.

The debate raged amongst scientists and politicians alike. Some argued for containment, for the control and weaponization of these newly empowered individuals. Others championed their rights, advocating for their protection and integration into society. But the fear, the uncertainty, and the potential for abuse of power loomed large over the discussion. The world had a difficult choice to make – to embrace the potential of this new generation or to fear and ultimately destroy it.

Anya, haunted by her visions, found herself increasingly drawn to the city, to the whispers of this hidden network. Kaspar, despite his fear and isolation, felt a growing sense of connection to the others, a sense of belonging that he'd never experienced before. They were not alone, and neither were the others who shared their gifts. Their journey would be fraught with peril, with challenges that tested their powers and their resilience. The echoes of the past served as a cautionary tale but also a source of strength, reminding them that they were not merely products of scientific manipulation but individuals with the power to shape their own destiny. The road ahead was long and treacherous, filled with the uncertainty of a future that held both immense potential and profound danger. The legacy of Tempête lived on, but this new generation had a choice: to succumb to the past or to forge a new future, one defined not by fear but by hope and the potential for a world where the extraordinary could coexist with the ordinary. The true outcome would depend on their choices.

The Ethical Debate Continues

The hushed whispers in the dimly lit Parisian cafes were not merely about Anya's visions or Kaspar's growing unease; they spoke of a deeper unease, a moral tremor echoing from the heart of Tempete's legacy. The creation of the enhanced individuals and the weaponization of human potential had sparked a firestorm of debate that raged across scientific and philosophical circles, a debate that had yet to find any semblance of resolution.

The initial public response had been one of stunned silence, quickly overtaken by a wave of fear and condemnation. The grotesque images of enhanced individuals, their powers twisted into instruments of war, haunted newspapers and fueled the anxieties of a world already reeling from the aftermath of global conflict. The public outcry was swift and brutal, demanding accountability and an end to such monstrous experiments. Governments, initially complicit in Tempete's activities, scrambled to distance themselves, issuing statements condemning the project and vowing to prevent similar atrocities in the future. International treaties were proposed, ambitious in scope but ultimately hampered by national interests and a lack of clear consensus on what constituted ethical genetic manipulation.

Within the scientific community, the debate was even more complex and fractured. Some scientists, horrified by Tempete's actions, called for a complete moratorium on all genetic enhancement research, arguing that the inherent risks far outweighed any potential benefits. They cited the unpredictable nature of genetic manipulation, the potential for unforeseen consequences, and the inherent danger of creating individuals with powers that could easily be misused. Their voices, passionate and well-intentioned, found a receptive audience among the public, further strengthening the calls for tighter regulations and greater oversight of scientific research.

Others, however, took a more nuanced stance, acknowledging the ethical concerns while simultaneously arguing for the potential benefits of genetic enhancement. They pointed to the potential for curing debilitating diseases, enhancing human capabilities in areas such as medicine and engineering, and even improving the human condition in ways previously unimaginable. They argued that the mistakes of Tempête were not inherent to the technology itself but rather a result of unchecked ambition and a lack of ethical oversight. They advocated for greater regulation, increased transparency, and the establishment of strict ethical guidelines to ensure that future genetic research was conducted responsibly and safely. Their arguments often fell on deaf ears, however, overshadowed by the public's lingering fear and distrust.

The most arguable aspect of the debate centered on the nature of humanity itself. If genetic enhancement could be used to eradicate disease and improve human capabilities, was it not our moral obligation to pursue it? But what about the potential for creating a genetically superior class of humans, widening the existing social and economic inequalities? What about the potential for creating individuals with powers so great that they could destabilize society? The very definition of humanity seemed to be at stake, with scientists, ethicists, and philosophers engaging in passionate and often hostile debates about the implications of altering the human genome. The lines blurred between scientific possibilities and moral responsibility, further complicating the discussion.

Adding another layer of complexity to the debate was the question of agency. Were the enhanced individuals, like Anya, Kaspar, and the others, merely victims of scientific manipulation, or did they possess the right to determine their own destiny? This question was particularly relevant to those who had escaped Tempete's clutches, individuals who found themselves haunted by their past and struggling to adapt to a world that viewed them with a mixture of fear and fascination. Their experiences challenged the notion that genetic manipulation was simply a scientific endeavor, highlighting the profound human cost associated with such ambitious projects.

The debate wasn't confined to the scientific and philosophical realms. It was divided into the political arena, becoming a battleground for competing ideologies and national interests. Governments struggled to balance the potential benefits of genetic enhancement with ethical concerns, leading to a patchwork of regulations that varied widely across countries and regions. Some nations embraced genetic research with enthusiasm, while others imposed strict restrictions, leading to international tensions and a lack of global cooperation. This political infighting only served to complicate the already fraught ethical landscape further, hindering any progress towards establishing a universally accepted framework for responsible genetic manipulation.

The legacy of Tempête also cast a long shadow over the debate. The experiments conducted within its walls, the brutal training endured by the enhanced individuals, and the tragic consequences that followed served as a stark reminder of the potential dangers of unchecked scientific ambition. The story of Tempête became a cautionary tale, a warning against the ethical pitfalls of prioritizing scientific advancement over human well-being. It was a story repeated in countless articles, books, and films, its imagery – the distorted faces of the enhanced individuals, the shadows of the clandestine laboratory – becoming ingrained in the collective consciousness.

Adding fuel to the fire was the ongoing mystery surrounding the missing memory serum. While leaked documents and scattered eyewitness accounts confirmed its existence, its precise composition and whereabouts remained unknown. The fear that it could fall into the wrong hands, potentially enabling widespread manipulation of memory and control, further intensified the debate. The serum itself became a symbol of the uncontrollable power of scientific advancement. This power could be used for good or evil, depending on the intentions of those who wielded it. This uncertainty fueled speculation and conspiracy theories, further complicating the already tense atmosphere.

The ethical debate surrounding Tempête and the broader implications of genetic manipulation were far from settled. It was a discussion that continued to evolve, shaped by new discoveries, technological advancements, and ongoing philosophical and political considerations. The future of genetic enhancement remained uncertain, a future fraught with both immense potential and profound risks. The choices made today, in terms of regulation, ethical guidelines, and international cooperation, would determine whether this powerful technology would be used to benefit humanity or to perpetuate its past mistakes. The echoes of Tempete's legacy would continue to resonate for generations to come, a constant reminder of the importance of responsible scientific practice and the enduring power of ethical considerations. The debate was not simply about science; it was about the very soul of humanity itself, and its future remained uncertain, hanging precariously in the balance. The question that lingered, unanswered and potentially unanswerable, was whether humanity was ready to shoulder the burden of such immense power. The answer, it seemed, was still being written, one ethical dilemma at a time.

A World Transformed

The world, once familiar with its rhythms and limitations, had irrevocably shifted. The whispers of Tempête, once confined to clandestine meetings and hushed conversations, had become a roar echoing across continents. The very fabric of society had been subtly, yet profoundly, altered. The air crackled with a new tension, a palpable awareness of unseen powers, of potential catastrophes lurking just beneath the surface.

The most immediate change was the rise of enhanced individuals – a phenomenon once relegated to science fiction, now a stark reality. Though the public remained largely unaware of the true extent of Tempete's work, the emergence of individuals displaying extraordinary abilities – inexplicable feats of strength, impossible acts of healing, or uncanny control over the elements – was undeniable. News reports spoke of "miracles" of "unprecedented recoveries," conveniently overlooking the darker implications behind these extraordinary events. Governments initially caught off guard, scrambled to understand and control this new reality, leading to a surge in clandestine programs mirroring, albeit on a smaller scale, the ruthless ambition of the original Tempête project.

The scientific community was divided. Some praised the breakthroughs, viewing the enhanced individuals as proof of humanity's limitless potential. Others, haunted by the moral transgressions of Tempête, called for a complete moratorium on genetic manipulation, warning of a dystopian future where the enhanced ruled over the unenhanced. This debate fueled a rapid evolution in ethical guidelines and regulations, though the speed of scientific advancement often outpaced the capacity for effective oversight.

The economic landscape also underwent a significant transformation. The demand for individuals with enhanced abilities, however limited or specialized, soared. Corporations, driven by profit, began investing heavily in genetic research, creating a new arms race for talent and technological dominance.

This created a lucrative black market for enhanced individuals, forcing many to live in the shadows, forever looking over their shoulders. The gap between the enhanced and the unenhanced widened, mirroring and even worsening existing social and economic inequalities.

Art and culture were profoundly affected. The emergence of enhanced individuals inspired a new wave of artistic expression, ranging from celebratory verses to cautionary tales. Novels, films, and paintings explored the complex themes of power, responsibility, and the very definition of humanity in a world forever changed by genetic manipulation. The enhanced themselves became figures of both fascination and fear, inspiring a complex mixture of awe and apprehension. Their presence permeated societal narratives, forcing a re-evaluation of traditional values and moral frameworks.

The legal system struggled to adapt to the new reality. Existing laws proved inadequate to deal with individuals possessing powers beyond the comprehension of ordinary courts. New legal frameworks were desperately needed, grappling with questions of accountability, justice, and the very definition of crime in a world where extraordinary abilities blurred the lines between intent and consequence. The creation of specialized courts and legal teams dedicated to handling cases involving enhanced individuals was a necessary, though imperfect, response.

The political landscape also experienced dramatic shifts. Governments grappled with the implications of enhanced individuals for national security. The potential for both defense and offense was immense, leading to a renewed arms race fueled by the desire to control and weaponize these extraordinary abilities. International treaties and agreements were desperately sought, but the inherent mistrust between nations, coupled with the potential for military advantage, hampered any real progress. The fear of a new world war fought not with conventional weapons but with enhanced individuals wielding devastating powers, hung heavily in the air.

Education transformed. New curricula were introduced, aimed at educating a generation aware of the possibilities and dangers of genetic enhancement. Ethical discussions and debates were integrated into the curriculum, encouraging critical thinking and responsible decision-making. The focus shifted towards developing a scientifically literate populace capable of discerning fact from fiction, and of making informed decisions in a world increasingly influenced by scientific advancements.

The very nature of warfare changed. The emergence of enhanced individuals transformed military strategies and tactics. Traditional notions of combat were rendered obsolete. The development of specialized units composed of enhanced individuals, coupled with the integration of advanced technology, made for a completely new style of military engagement. The implications for international security were profound and far-reaching.

The psychological impact was equally profound. The existence of enhanced individuals challenged fundamental notions of human identity and potential. People struggled to reconcile their traditional beliefs and values with a reality that defied expectations. Anxiety and fear were widespread, fueled by the uncertainties of the future. The need for psychological support and counseling soared, leading to a new focus on mental health, particularly amongst the enhanced individuals themselves, who often struggled to adapt to their unique capabilities.

In the shadows of this transformed world, the echoes of Tempete's original sin continued to reverberate. The legacy of the underground project, once a hushed secret, now cast a long shadow over the future, a constant reminder of the potential for unchecked scientific ambition to unleash unforeseen consequences. The question remained: could humanity learn from its past mistakes, or was it destined to repeat them, creating new horrors in its relentless pursuit of progress? The answer was as elusive as the wind, a riddle yet to be deciphered in the turbulent landscape of a world forever changed. The moral compass spun wildly, its needle pointing to an uncertain future, one where the boundaries between human and superhuman blurred into an ever-shifting landscape. The fight for the soul of humanity, for the very definition of what it meant to be human, had just begun.

Irina's Warning

The flickering gaslight cast long, dancing shadows across Irina's face, highlighting the sharp angles of her cheekbones and the intensity in her usually calm eyes. She sat hunched over a chipped porcelain teacup, the steam rising like a fragile ghost in the dimly lit attic room. Outside, the Parisian rain lashed against the windowpanes, a relentless percussion mirroring the turmoil within her. Across from her, Thomas, his enhanced senses straining to pick up every nuance of her expression, remained silent, a statue carved from granite and shadowed by guilt.

"They don't understand," Irina finally whispered, her voice barely audible above the storm's fury. "They think they control us, that they can harness our…abilities…for their own twisted ends. But they're playing with fire, Thomas. A fire they can't hope to contain."

Thomas shifted the barely perceptible creak of the ancient floorboards a testament to his superhuman strength carefully restrained. He knew what she meant. He had tasted the bitterness of their control, felt the chilling weight of his training, the relentless pressure to obey. He'd spent five years hunting down his former colleagues, haunted by the faces of those he'd been forced to hurt, the echoes of their screams still ringing in his heightened ears.

"The serum…the memory serum," Irina continued, her gaze drifting to the rain-streaked window. "It's a terrifying Band-Aid on a gaping wound. They think they've erased the past, erased their culpability. But the past has a way of returning, Thomas. It always does."

Her words hung in the air, heavy with foreboding. She had seen glimpses of the future, fragmented visions that sent shivers down her spine, visions of a world irrevocably altered by Tempete's legacy. Visions not just of superhuman conflict, but of something far more insidious, a manipulation of the very fabric of reality.

"They're already trying to repeat it," she said, her voice taking on a sharper edge. "Dr. Reed…he hasn't given up. He believes he can refine the process and create…more of us. Better ones. But he doesn't see the price. He doesn't see the potential for catastrophic failure."

Irina leaned forward, her eyes blazing with an unsettling intensity. "The enhancements, Thomas, they aren't just physical changes. They're alterations to the very core of our being. They unravel the delicate balance of the nature of humanity itself. Each success, each new mutant, it's like a crack in the foundation of reality. And with each crack, the instability grows."

She paused, taking a trembling sip of her tea. The silence that followed was punctuated only by the relentless drumming of the rain. Thomas, despite his enhanced senses, felt a chilling emptiness settle in his heart, a premonition of something vast and terrible.

"They talk of progress, of advancement," Irina continued, her voice low and bitter. "But progress without ethics, without understanding the consequences...that's not progress, Thomas. It's self-destruction. It's the prelude to annihilation."

Her words echoed the anxieties that had been gnawing at him for years. His enhanced senses had made him acutely aware of the world's fragility, its delicate balance easily shattered. He had seen the subtle shifts in the global order, the growing unease, the underlying current of fear. He had felt the ripple effect of Tempete's actions, the unforeseen consequences of their hubris.

"They don't see the ripple effects," she whispered, her voice almost a sigh. "The unintended consequences. They're blinded by their ambition, by their thirst for power. They crave control, but in the end, they'll lose everything."

She described scenarios and horrifying visions drawn from her unique perspective. She spoke of mutations spiraling out of control, of unforeseen powers emerging, powers far exceeding anything Tempête had ever imagined. She described a world where the line between human and superhuman blurred beyond recognition, a world teetering on the brink of chaos.

She spoke of ecological disasters and unforeseen consequences of the alterations to the human genome that rippled through the environment, causing catastrophic shifts in weather patterns, mass extinctions, and unpredictable mutations in the animal kingdom. She painted a grim picture of a world ravaged by unchecked scientific ambition, a world where the very air was poisoned, the earth scorched, and humanity itself on the verge of extinction.

She spoke of societal collapse, the breakdown of order caused by fear and mistrust, a world consumed by paranoia and prejudice, where superhumans were hunted down and persecuted, and where ordinary humans lived in constant fear of the unknown. The visions were terrifyingly realistic, imbued with the painful weight of her prophetic insights.

"They've created a monster, Thomas," she said, her voice breaking slightly. "And that monster isn't just us. It's the unchecked ambition, the thirst for power, the disregard for the consequences. It's the very nature of their pursuit, their unbridled faith in progress without morality."

She spoke of the subtle ways in which the world had changed, the creeping sense of unease that permeated society, the underlying fear of the unknown, and the growing divide between those who held power and those who did not. She spoke of governments secretly funding clandestine projects, attempting to replicate Tempete's success, oblivious to the potential consequences. She described a future where humanity's own creations would rise up against them, a chilling prophecy born from the tragic legacy of Tempête.

The rain outside continued its relentless assault, mirroring the storm raging within Irina. She spoke of the ethical implications of their existence, the moral burden they carried, and the responsibility they had to prevent the catastrophic future she foresaw. It was a warning, a desperate plea to halt the relentless march of scientific progress before it consumed them all.

"We are a warning," she concluded, her voice barely a whisper. "A testament to the dangers of unchecked ambition. We are the echoes of their past, and the harbingers of their future. They must learn from our mistakes, Thomas, before it's too late."

Thomas, hardened by years of brutal training and the weight of his actions, felt a cold fear grip him. He had seen the monstrous potential of Tempete's experiments firsthand, and Irina's words painted a future far more terrifying than anything he had previously imagined. The weight of responsibility, the burden of his past, pressed down upon him heavier than ever before. The echoes of Tempete's past were not just whispers anymore; they were the thunder of an impending storm, and the question remained: could they, could anyone, stop it?

The Uncertain Future

The rain continued its relentless assault on the attic window, a rhythmic counterpoint to the silence that had settled between Irina and Thomas. The fragile peace, born of shared trauma and a desperate need for understanding, felt precarious, a thin sheet of ice over a chasm of unresolved guilt and fear. Irina finally broke the silence, her voice a low murmur that barely carried above the storm.

"They won't stop," she said, her gaze fixed on the swirling patterns in her tea. "Reed… he believes in their work. He believes it can be perfected, that the failures were merely…adjustments needed. He sees a future where…where Tempete's creations are not hunted but celebrated."

Thomas shivered, not from the cold seeping through the cracked windowpanes but from the chill that snaked through his very being at her words. The image of Dr. Reed, his face a mask of unwavering conviction, rose in his memory. He had seen the doctor's relentless pursuit of progress, a relentless march fueled by a blind faith in science that disregarded the human cost. That chilling dedication was far more terrifying than any of the powers unleashed by Tempête.

"He's wrong," Thomas rasped, his voice rough with the weight of his past. "This…this isn't progress. It's a monster we unleashed, and it can't be controlled."

Irina nodded slowly, her eyes distant, haunted by visions only she could see. "The serum… the memory-erasing serum. Dubois, Moreau, Petrova… they thought it would erase the guilt, the horror. But it didn't. It only buried it, buried it deep, leaving behind a vacant space filled with…something else. Something unsettling. Something…empty."

She traced the rim of her teacup with a trembling finger, her voice barely audible. "I remember fragments, flashes of light and shadow, the smell of ozone and… fear. The fear isn't gone. It's just…different. More diffuse, more pervasive. A constant hum beneath the surface of my consciousness." She paused, her breath hitching slightly. "What if Reed's work… what if he finds a way to create more? What if he finds a way to perfect these…enhancements? To control them?"

The implication hung heavily in the air, unspoken yet understood. The possibility of an army of enhanced individuals, controlled by a man consumed by his ambition, was a chilling prospect. A weapon far more powerful, far more terrifying, than any conventional army.

Thomas knew instinctively that Irina's fears were justified. He had seen the raw power of the Tempête creations, the sheer destructive capacity they possessed. He had felt the crushing weight of his own enhanced abilities, the constant struggle to control the instincts instilled within him during his years of brutal training. He had hunted his former comrades, driven by a loyalty he no longer understood, haunted by the faces of those he had killed. The memory of Elara's agonized scream as his enhanced strength had shattered her ribs, the lingering image of Seraphina's terrified eyes as he'd silenced her telepathic cries clawed at his conscience.

"We need to stop him," Thomas said, his voice firm, a newfound resolve hardening his features. The years of training, the relentless pursuit, the burden of guilt – all of it merged into a single, unwavering purpose. He wouldn't let Reed unleash another wave of destruction upon the world.

But how? The question hung unanswered, a specter of doubt that threatened to unravel their fragile hope. They were fugitives, hunted by a relentless military machine, haunted by their past, and desperately outnumbered. Reed had the resources of the military, the support of those who saw their work as progress, and a chilling determination that transcended morality.

"We have to find the others," Irina said, her voice stronger now, infused with a newfound determination. "Marcus, Elara… even Seraphina. Together… perhaps we have a chance."

Finding the others would be a daunting task. Years had passed since they had escaped from the clutches of the military. Their lives were scattered, their identities concealed, their very existence a secret whispered only in the shadows. Tracking them down would require a network of contacts, an understanding of the hidden currents beneath the surface of society, a level of subtlety that Thomas, hardened by his years of ruthless efficiency, had almost forgotten how to achieve. The thought of reaching out to those who had betrayed their trust was repugnant, but the urgency of the situation, the impending threat from Reed's relentless pursuit, left no room for hesitation.

The next few months were a blur of secret meetings, coded messages, and desperate searches. Irina, with her unparalleled intellect, proved invaluable in tracking down the elusive remnants of Tempete's experiments. Her network of contacts within the scientific community, cultivated over years of living in hiding, provided crucial leads. Thomas, his enhanced senses straining to the limit, detected subtle clues others would have missed, weaving together fragmented information into a coherent pattern.

Slowly, painstakingly, they located Marcus, his pyrokinetic abilities suppressed, living a solitary life in a remote village in the Pyrenees. Elara, her weather manipulation dulled by years of self-imposed isolation, was found working as a farmhand in the vast, windswept plains of Ukraine. The search for Seraphina proved the most challenging. Her telepathic abilities made her incredibly elusive, leaving only faint, fragmented traces in the minds of those who had unwittingly crossed her path.

Bringing them together proved to be an even greater challenge. Each carried their own scars, their own burdens, their own deep-seated distrust of the others. The years of isolation and the trauma of their shared past had erected walls of suspicion and fear between them. The task of rebuilding their fractured trust, of forging a fragile alliance against a common enemy, seemed insurmountable. But the looming threat of Reed's ambition drove them forward, a shared sense of dread uniting them in a desperate, uneasy alliance.

The final piece of their puzzle – a chance to stop Reed – came in the form of a cryptic message from a disillusioned member of Reed's team. The message alluded to a new project, an even more ambitious undertaking than the creation of super-powered mutants. This project threatened to unleash a catastrophe far greater than any they could have imagined. This message spoke of a weapon, a weapon unlike any the world had ever seen, the culmination of Reed's relentless pursuit of perfection.

The message indicated a specific location, a hidden laboratory deep within the Alps. This was their only chance, their last hope to stop Reed before his horrifying ambitions could become reality. The battle that awaited them would be a desperate struggle for survival, not only against Reed and his scientific advancements but also against the demons of their own past. The echoes of Tempete's past were not just whispers anymore; they were a roar, a storm of their own making, threatening to consume them all. The uncertain future hung heavy in the air, fraught with danger and the chilling weight of their collective responsibility. The past had consequences, and the future would be forged in the fires of their choices.